Backlash Bounty

by

Lori Power

McGuire Series, Book 3

Backlash Bounty

Cover Art by *Debbie Taylor*

The Wild Rose Press, Inc.
PO Box 708
Adams Basin, NY 14410-0708
Visit us at www.thewildrosepress.com

Publishing History
First Edition, 2022
Trade Paperback ISBN 978-1-5092-4056-2
Digital ISBN 978-1-5092-4057-9

McGuire Series, Book 3
Published in the United States of America

Dedication

For all my family at "home"

Author's Note

Every war—every battle—has winners and losers, but more importantly *perspective*.

The War of 1812 technically began June 18th, 1812, when war was declared, and ended with the Treaty of Ghent, signed in December 1814 but formalized February 18, 1815.

However, many historians attest the main body of the war occurred during four months in 1814.

The two theatres of war involved land and sea and included the British, Americans, Canadians, and Native peoples of many tribes and standing.

Again, perspective.

Americans may view the war as a "second war of independence," this time against the reign of the British Empire, bringing the true birth of American freedom and the founding of the Union; however, for the British, this war was forgettable, an adjunct to their longstanding conflicts with France.

As Britain required crews for their navy in the Napoleonic wars, they used a policy of "impressment," forcing approximately 10,000 American sailors into service. Though American politicians fought against this measure, it didn't prevent a thousand American ships getting seized in the blockades the British set against France. It should be noted, though, that the majority of these sailors were in fact British subjects and therefore subject to British laws of desertion.

The blockades and subsequent seizures promoted the growth of illicit trade, especially along the St. Lawrence River—the border between Canada and the United States.

Garrett lifted the light and glanced around the claustrophobic interior. Then his breath sailed from his body and he felt an almost giddy surge. "There, MacLeod." He pointed along the length of wall, observing the grotto wasn't nearly as small as he'd first thought. He was again the small boy who stole into the secret vault of their family to be dazzled by the jewels contained therein.

Measuring his step, he strode the length of wall that unless inspected properly looked as though it were the end of the line. Yet it wasn't. Up close, stalagmites met stalactites as teeth along a jawline. Retrieving the light, he felt between the white columns, pushing until one broke and he could wedge his way into the mouth.

Water sloshed above the top of his boot. "More light."

Brian complied, holding the torch aloft while he followed through the gnashing jaws of rock. The sudden light in the gloom gave Garrett a wide view of what lay within and what would have been missed had they not had the map.

"By the Lord Jesus, this will end 'er."

Praise for Lori Power

"Lori Power is putting together a very readable series that merges the rough and readiness of life at sea and on the New World frontier with the gentility and manners of the aristocracy of the period."

~Grant Leishma, Readers' Favorite

~

"I loved the plot as it prioritized love and gave women the voices to do and be."

~Jennifer Ibiam, Readers' Favorite

~

"The author takes a different stance with her characters as they don't fit the usual British nobles during the Napoleonic Era, adding a fascinating twist."

~Peggy Jo Wipf, Readers' Favorite

~

"A delightful period romance that leaves me with a smile and a heart full of thanks for stumbling across this gem."

~Lisa McCombs, Readers' Favorite

Canadians view the War of 1812 as the cornerstone when the country became a nation unto itself. Heroes of note include Shawnee chief Tecumseh, who lost his life defending upper Canada against hostile Americans. The bravery of women looms large in this account of historical details and features women of service on the battlefield—women like Laura Secord, who struggled through almost twenty miles of swampland to warn troops of an imminent attack.

Truly, the end of the war was the abdication of Napoleon in April 1814. From then on, securing a peaceful, stable, and durable settlement on the continent was featured prominently by politicians on all sides. The Treaty of Ghent was an agreement to hold to the status quo.

Chapter One

1813, Capraia Isola

Garrett McGuire straightened and stretched his back. The creaks and cracks offered a welcome relief from the toil. He took the bandana from his neck and mopped his streaming brow. Strands of his hair had come loose from his queue and clung to his face like dark webs.

Members of his crew, stooped from their combined labor, followed his lead. They rested in various poses, wiping blood and sweat on trouser legs and arms of their shirts. Many used their shoulder as a sponge for the perspiration on their brow. Even for those used to the physical labor aboard ship, this environment came with a different variation of harshness.

He glanced down at his own sea-hardened hands, bloodied from trying to move the volcanic rocks blocking the cavern they wished to enter. Despite having wrapped their hands with strips of leather to protect as much as they could, they found their precaution created little armor. The razorlike edges sliced shallow seams through the callouses. The fluid pearled but didn't run, and it stung in the saltwater.

First Mate Brian MacLeod, brother to Garrett's beloved wife, Bessy, leaned a shoulder against the boulder and pierced him with a knowing stare, then nodded. Never one for the gab, MacLeod swiped the rag from his head to wipe the rillettes of perspiration. His normally light red-brown hair appeared near black with the damp. The man retied his bandana and smiled at Garrett, revealing a gap in the crooked array of teeth. "Does this mean we're officially pirates now, Capt'in?"

Garrett arched his arms high above his head and rolled his neck first one way and then the other. Squinting against the glare of the sun, he looked out over the small harbor where his ship, the *Isle Sky*, bobbed at anchor, while he contemplated his answer. The island of Elba lay just visible as a purple streak on the horizon.

From anyone else, the mention of "pirate" might have grazed a nerve. The pursuit of treasure had started his family's legacy when his father met his mother and then uncovered the loot from Oak Island, in the Americas. Though many might guess, they had never confirmed the rumors, nor did Garrett intend ever to reveal the family secret. This kind of notoriety was something he would prefer not to carry in the normal course of business. Yet he suspected that had those rumors not existed, he might not be here at this time at his majesty's pleasure.

Without hesitation, Garrett found an easy smile and shook his head, scratching the scruff of beard he hadn't tended to in many days. "No." He stretched the word, feeling for the length of their voyage, they'd been on a fool's errand. Despite their lifelong friendship and being a brother by marriage, Garrett would not confirm what Brian presumed.

At this point, for this task, Brian knew all. How much to reveal openly to the crew at large would depend on what they found. Provided the intel was correct. To come so far without booty for payment wouldn't make for happy men. They were well used to a percentage of all they bartered between the two sides. But there was no need for decision now. He'd consider later what to do about that, and their next moves, should this prove an empty excursion.

"No," he repeated, feeling the strength rather than the uncertainty of the word this time. "This 'ere's British soil. Been so since '96 under Admiral Nelson. Today we work for the crown's pleasure. We stop only when we find what we set out to discover."

Though the directions to the island had been received covertly, care of Cornwallis out of Halifax, they were clear and precise. What might amount to nothing required inspecting, to be sure. He had been so entrusted because he'd been running successful clandestine trade operations for the last eighteen months, alternating between the British and those fledgling Americans. Everyone got their share without deceit. Who would win this American feud wouldn't be determined by him. On behalf of his family, his goal was to ensure they were well placed for either outcome.

Garrett's gaze traveled the length of the rocky beach, then scanned the horizon for a telltale mast. The last thing he needed now was competition or discovery. Weariness had become a faithful friend on this mission. By its very nature, as it stood outside their normal merchant activities, this consignment was very different. Even though he knew Cornwallis had assigned this mission based on the rumors of his father, Mackenzie McGuire, still he had no confidence in the outcome. The age of the map, the location of the island, the fact that the admiral clearly had never found what he and his crew now sought—all troubled Garrett as no other assignment had troubled him before.

His men, loyal and well-paid, followed him without question, MacLeod being his only confidant to the extent of knowing what they sought. Spanish treasure. He certainly had no allegiance to anything Spanish and took great personal joy in stripping Spanish ships of any bounty, whatever that may be. He shook his head at the incredulity of the very notion of favoritism and the irony that his family's fortune started when Mackenzie seized a Spanish ship. Something whispered in his doubting mind that surely all treasure worth finding had already been found.

"Not so much pleasure today," Brian replied, curling a length of rope over his arm. "'Tis a lonesome island, to be sure. Not fit for man, barely survivable by the few beasts hereabouts. Whatever they think is here—"

Garrett clamped a hand on the man's upper arm. "Waste of time, I'm sure, MacLeod." He lowered his voice, then winked. "Nor do I think our sovereign expects anything. But war is expensive, my friend. Finding this before Napoleon does will either alter the course or confirm the old abbot was as crazy as his jailers suspected."

"Big risk for a waste of time," said Ruddy Roddy, one of the ten trusted men he'd allowed to come ashore. He sat close enough to hear the first but not the last of Garrett's comments. "I sees Italy. If we're not on our way with the next tide, we're sure to be spotted by the Frenchies patrolling from Marseille."

"On that I can agree," said Garrett, reaching for the

rope dangling from MacLeod's thick forearm. "Best to be done and on our way, eh, men?"

With murmured groans but no complaints, they rose and re-formed their two groups. While the men worked the lever under the boulder, he and MacLeod pushed the rope around the edges. The wild goats, scattered at their arrival, had returned to their grazing, seemingly no longer viewing the seamen as a threat. He smiled at this. The periodic bleats reminded Garrett that, if nothing else, they'd have fresh meat for their efforts.

"Be lively, lads," he encouraged.

He and Brian criss-crossed the cord around the back of the rock. "Okay, that'll do for a moment," he commanded. "Now to the ropes."

Leaving the lengths of cable in place, they dug deep beneath the stone. The two lines formed along each end of the rope and began to heave until they felt the great weight give way. Though it might only have been fractional, it was enough to re-energize their efforts.

"To the top now, Spider." Garrett shouted to the wiry dwarf-like man who, on a normal day at sea, could scale a mainsail mast like an insect. "Use your legs and push."

Encouraged by the sudden movement of the great weight, they worked as a unit until the mass rolled from its historic foundation a few inches along the jimmies.

"Heave," MacLeod bellowed. "Put yur backs into it."

"I can see inside," Spider yelled.

"Enough," Garrett bawled. "Stay as you are. Hold tight. Don't let this massive bastard retake its hold in the foundation." He turned to Ruddy Roddy. "The light. Quick, man."

The young man scrambled away and returned just as quickly with the lantern, already lit.

The skin of Garrett's bare back tore as he squeezed his large form through the narrow entrance. Although he winced, he didn't pause. Stale air, damp and aged, filled his lungs. Here was a grave if ever there was.

Brian followed, pushing at the immovable mass to lever his wide shoulders within. Garrett could hear his companion's skin being punctured by the rock shards.

"Hold this burly piece of Mother Earth, boys. It'll not make me day to be trapped inside," Brian growled before dipping his head to clear the small mouth, a rush torch in his outstretched hand.

With just the two of them in the cavity, Garrett laid the oil lamp on the damp stone at his feet and stooped to retrieve the ancient map from his boot. His stomach clenched and anticipation flared. The entrance was exactly as the map described. "Three paces from where the teeth mesh."

"What could that mean?" Brian stooped nearer the flame to peer at the markings on the map.

Garrett lifted the light and glanced around the claustrophobic interior. Then his breath sailed from his body and he felt an almost giddy surge. "There, MacLeod." He pointed along the length of wall, observing the grotto wasn't nearly as small as he'd first thought. He was again the small boy who stole into the secret vault of their family to be dazzled by the jewels contained therein.

Measuring his step, he strode the length of wall that unless inspected properly looked as though it were the end of the line. Yet it wasn't. Up close, stalagmites met stalactites as teeth along a jawline. Retrieving the light, he felt between the white columns, pushing until one broke and he could wedge his way into the mouth.

Water sloshed above the top of his boot. "More light."

Brian complied, holding the torch aloft while he followed through the gnashing jaws of rock. The sudden light in the gloom gave Garrett a wide view of what lay within and what would have been missed had they not had the map.

"By the Lord Jesus, this will end 'er."

Chapter Two

1813, Boston

Bessy signed her full name. It felt strange to write a name she now so seldom used. The pen seemed leaden as she wrote "Anne Elizabeth MacLeod McGuire" with a weighted heart. She could hardly remember who that person was now. Since her marriage to Garrett, fifteen years ago, it was only in letters that she seemed to exist in this formal context, and even then the name conjured an image of a young girl wandering lost until she found Garrett.

For this life in the New World with her husband, children, brother, and his family, these last years, she'd willingly become Garrett's "Bessy." Even her brother, teasing at first, adopted the moniker. Though she had resisted anyone but Garrett refer to her as Bessy when they'd first wed, when everyone seemed to refuse to introduce her in any other way, she quickly tired of the explanation and adjusted and grew into the name, the role, and her new life. Now, she was forever more Elizabeth McGuire, or just Bessy.

These wayward thoughts served only to distract for a moment. She sighed. Then, straightening, she brushed away the moisture in her eyes, thinking of Garrett. How she missed his conversation, his touch, his… He had to be alive. No, she would not entertain any other thoughts. He and Brian both had to be alive, and that was that. She could not become sidetracked.

Resolutely, she folded the parchment, melted the wax, and sealed the missive with her father's ring. The MacLeod insignia of "hold fast" woven within the bull, the belt, the rope, and the buckle. The meaning couldn't have been more profound in this instance.

Done. She stroked the smooth paper. If something were to happen, Bessy's sister Beverly would send the inheritance for both Bessy and Brian for the care of their children—her boys and Brian's girls—and ensure Marie-Kelly MacLeod, Brian's wife, was provided for, regardless of whether she returned to England or chose to stay on this side of the great ocean.

Bessy stood and passed the letter to Marie-Kelly, her sister by marriage. Though no one could ever replace Beverly, Marie-Kelly had become a sister of her heart. In fact, unlike Bevvy's golden locks, Marie-Kelly's dark red hair meant she and Bessy could, and often did, pass for blood siblings.

Bessy bit her lip to keep it from wobbling. Could she do this? Really. Of course, she had to. Bessy pressed both hands to her abdomen and forced a shaky breath in, then out. In a better world, she wouldn't have to wonder about the long-term security of her children. But this world had become anything but safe these last years.

The two women had planned this. Marie-Kelly nodded the once, understanding, and stashed the envelope while Bessy stripped down to her shift before the crackling fire. Quelling the quake in her stomach, Bessy fixed a resolute stare ahead. As her most trusted friend, Marie-Kelly was the only woman she would leave in charge of her children while embarking on such a journey.

"Are ye ready?" Marie-Kelly asked softly, lifting the scissors.

Bessy knelt on the hard planked floor and removed the pins from her russet colored hair, allowing the mass of curls to cascade this one last time. As still as a statue she tried not to listen as the blades sheared close to her scalp. She closed her eyes to stop the view of the heavy locks falling to the floor.

Marie-Kelly laid her hand upon Bessy's shoulder and squeezed. They hadn't spoken. In these wee hours before the dawn, while everyone seemed to be asleep, the two women shared all that couldn't be spoken.

Refusing to indulge in self-pity, she bowed her head once, then tipped back on her toes. Rising to her feet and drawing a shuddered breath, Bessy turned back to the mirror and touched the orb of her shorn head. She couldn't recognize the person staring back. This person's eyes consumed the pale face. Yes, all the features matched, but somehow in the last moments she had changed. Twisting slightly, she bent to help Marie-Kelly pick up the last of the hair and drop it onto the blaze. The sizzle and scent made her stomach churn uncomfortably.

The women lived side by side, but as their husbands were frequently away, they often shared communal duties in rearing their children in a large extended family. While Marie-Kelly's girls were nestled in her bed, her two boys also slept on and did not have to bear witness to their mother's transformation. Let the children assume she tended the sick and the wounded returning to the city. They were used to her being called away to aid the ailing. Only she and Marie-Kelly would know the extent of her planned travels this day.

Bessy shook her head decisively. In these fledgling states, war brought more than bullets to kill people.

The women faced one another, and Marie-Kelly's shoulders began to shake. "My good sister, you cannot." Tears streamed down her cheeks. "'Tis too dangerous."

Bessy set the scissors on the mantel before running her palm over the coarse cut. "We've decided, have we not?" The pads of her fingers encountered uneven lengths, stubbly in some areas. There was no time for tears. They had agreed. Too much needed to be done before dawn. "It must be me. I have an excuse to travel, and my healer's bag affords me some protection."

Marie-Kelly blinked rapidly, and her eyes cleared. Then the dark brown orbs turned as hard as mahogany. "We cannot know this for sure. You are traveling into the depths—"

"No one must know where I go, Marie, my dearest." Bessy stepped to the dresser, retrieved one of the money purses, then returned to take Marie's icy fingers in her own. She balanced the weight between their clasped hands. "You keep this on you at all times. We don't know when and on what little notice you may have to flee the city. You are my most trusted companion. I leave you in charge. Promise me, Marie, on the lives of our bairns. Promise me."

Marie-Kelly straightened and pulled her shoulders back and smiled, the small gap between her front teeth endearing. "You can depend on me, sister," she said, the familiar steel threading her thick Scottish brogue.

11

"On the lives of my children, I will keep your secret, reporting you too ill to visit to all who inquire, until you return."

Bessy swallowed and forced the words. "And if I do not…"

She couldn't finish the sentence. Too impossible to think she would never see her boys, Malcolm and Mack, again.

Marie-Kelly pulled her into a hard embrace. "I will send word to the MacLeod, now settled on the island of Cape Breton off New Scotland…oh, that we may one day join our clan again, sister. Be they better days."

"Indeed."

Though she and Brian also shared the MacLeod name, their father, Gerald, had raised them English. While she and Garrett were sorting the marriage contract, Brian had gone in search of his roots, where he met and fell in love with Marie-Kelly from the Isle of Skye. Brian had been Garrett's lifelong companion and was first mate on his ship, so without hesitation, once married, they had joined Bessy and Garrett when they decided to settle in Boston nearly fifteen years earlier. Marie-Kelly was always amused by Garrett's ship being named after her place of birth. Her uncle had also come to this New World, later, but had settled north, outside the union of the states.

Now Marie-Kelly squeezed her wrists, wrenching Bessy back to the present.

"Seems Boston is no home for us any longer, Marie. In this colonial war where brothers and sisters are pitted against one another, there is no room for those unwilling to take a side. This is not a 'we versus them.' " Bessy bowed her head, which now felt too light for the rest of her body—it gave her the impression of floating. How could anyone decide on sides? Which party wins—the British—the French—the Americans—those who owned the land first, before any of those? For her, this was not a coin decision but a hexagon, to be sure, with so many players and each with their own politics attached. "To think we have not learned from the wars which drove us here in the first place."

"A crying shame."

Bessy raised her gaze to meet her friend's. "You'll see my boys get there safe?"

"Oh, I canna face it." Marie-Kelly glanced to the cracked ceiling, sniffed, and shook her head. Her eyes shone, but the tears did not spill. The moisture reflected like gold in the firelight. Then her forehead gently met Bessy's. "I will be waiting for ye there. For thee, fair sister, I will. I will ensure the children are awaiting for ye and our men."

Bessy pulled Marie-Kelly into a fierce hug. "We are one mother now, Marie. Hear me. My bairns, your bairns. For all of ours. Together."

One of Garrett's men, Horace, had returned two days previous, limping, arm in a makeshift sling, a skeleton of the man he'd been when they left months previous on a mission to which Garrett had alluded only vaguely regarding its significance. The women were used to these long absences at sea, their men always spending equal or more time on land these last years. Letters and missives kept the families informed. But the ship had been long overdue, and the arrival of Horace heralded bad news. Sure enough, he confirmed the ship had been captured while running contraband back down the coast to Boston from Halifax.

According to Horace and the few crew that had managed to escape, Garrett had been captured. He'd refused to abandon his ship until all hands were off. Concerning was that there was no further word of Brian and the remaining crew members. While Bessy dreaded to think of her husband in captivity, at least she knew something. Her heart ached with the unknown whereabouts of her brother and Marie-Kelly's staunch belief that he too was on his way back to her.

In the intervening weeks it had taken Horace to return to Boston, Garrett could have been taken anywhere. Likely Brian and the remaining crew might have been captured as well. Yet Bessy surmised that, due to their rank and negotiating tools, Garrett and Brian would be worth more alive and at least somewhat well. Knowing roughly what they had been after, Bessy knew that if they had been successful, the value of loot would mean a lot to fund the war effort of whatever side held him at present.

Bessy couldn't know her exact destination. It would have to be a naval base. "I will find them. No matter how far or how long."

"I know you will."

Stepping lightly, the women gathered the clothes and provisions, including an old pair of Mack's breeches, rolled and then roped at the waist to fit. Despite being only fourteen this year and eager for his chance to prove himself a man at sea like his father and uncle, her son's clothes swam on Bessy's slight frame. Malcolm too, now twelve, showed signs of the strapping man to come. Built tall and broad of shoulder like his father, the boy outgrew his clothing quickly.

She would utilize an outgrown shirt, then a pair of her youngest's old boots to fit her small feet.

Marie-Kelly unrolled the soft length of cotton fabric, while Bessy raised her arms. "'Tis a good thing you don't have my ample bosom." Marie smiled. "I doubt any length of strong fabric would hide their bounce."

Glad of the respite from the tension, Bessy grinned. "Your figure has always been the envy of many a woman around these parts," she agreed, nodding her head. "Though I too in my youth would have paid dearly for such a fine form. You are like my beloved Beverly in that, I being more comfortable with my herbs. Today, however, you are correct. I am thankful for my flat angles." She followed Marie's movements with her eyes while the woman tied the ends together. "Yet a wee bit more height would help to pull off the disguise."

"No denying it, dear one." Marie-Kelly pursed her lips. "But there is nothing for it now." Her gaze glided over Bessy's shorn head. "We are committed. You will be a medicine man."

Moments later, Bessy pulled the tricorn hat tight over her brow and picked up the other coin purse. "You know where I hid the remainder of the money?"

"Under the floor board in the children's room. Second from the window, under the crib."

Bessy bowed her head and pinched the bridge of her nose to stem further emotion. The lump in her throat grew to consume her breath. Little Beverly, named for her sister, hadn't survived her first year, taken by the fever rampant in the city. Now a year since her baby's death, she still could not bear to put the crib into storage.

Having been fortunate to conceive after three miscarried babies in the intervening years since Malcolm's healthy delivery, Bessy suspected this babe was her last. Despite herself, she often found herself lost in thought, hovering over the empty bed, fingering the pink embroidered coverlet. Her beautiful daughter, taken like so many she couldn't save over the winter.

Marie-Kelly gripped her shoulders, pale face blotched with color. "You will have another."

Never another little Beverly, but Bessy nodded anyway, knowing better. Now was not the time. "God willing."

Turning, she took the knife from the mantel, removed it from the sheath, and tested the blade against the hair of her arm. Sharp enough to shave smooth. Replacing the blade, she bent to lace it to her calf, where it would lie just inside her boot. Marie-Kelly provided the second knife, which they attached to her wrist. Their warm breaths mingled, though they refrained from speaking. Finally the pistol, primed and ready, was lashed to her belt.

Marie-Kelly moved to retrieve the blanket sack filled with all the provisions they could muster on such short notice. "God speed, dearest sister."

Chapter Three

Garrett McGuire held no title of interest to his captors—none they could trace without considerable investigation. Black Mack, through his vast contacts, had seen to that personally. Garrett's ship had been a ghost in these waters for the duration of the war…until now. Somehow word of what he'd been tasked to find had circulated. Turncoats formerly loyal to Cornwallis revealed what they knew, though he doubted the depth of their knowledge or if they could do other than suspect he'd been successful.

It was only fortunate that they had been running high in the water, having already dispatched their freight in safe harbors. Timing and weather—heavy fog suddenly clearing—had been unfortunate, leading to their capture.

Now, his one known possession, the *Isle Sky*, floated nearby, controlled by former allies, while they searched for information to confirm their suspicions. These confederate jailors considered him and his men enemies, and measured them as traitors. The location of the dropped consignment formed the only reason he still drew breath. He scanned the faces of the two other men confined with him. He need not even communicate to either Brian or Ruddy Roddy, his most loyal trusted mates, that the moment any of them gave over the whereabouts of the treasure would be the moment when their lives would end, their value finished as sure as if he fired the bullet himself.

He hoped the majority of crew who were not captured with him had managed to escape to safety. They knew where to gather. Like any crew, they had a contingency plan. But the landscape was a minefield of battles and skirmishes, and they'd have a long way to go overland to gather help and take action.

"On your feet, rabble," shouted the uniformed guard from the open doorway. "Lieutenant Samuel Holden enters."

The shuffle and crinkle of stiff fabrics followed this announcement, punctuated by groans of pain. Other than his immediate crew, many if not all the prisoners in Garrett's cell were either wounded from nearby battles or injured as a result of the events of capture.

Reluctant to evacuate the choice spot next to the wall, but seeing no other option, Garrett braced his weight on an arm before rolling onto his side and making his way, heavily, to his feet. Gritting his teeth, he tried to ignore the stabbing pains in his right calf and his ribcage.

"You are all antagonists of the state. You chose to side with a foreign country against its patriots." Lieutenant Samuel Holden stepped farther into the cell and glared at each inmate directly. His furrowed brow, craggy face, and snakelike eyes intended to intimidate.

Twenty men in various states of health and dress stared back. Brian and Ruddy Roddy flanked Garrett.

At first, Holden's erect stance and barrel chest gave the impression of a mutton-chopped giant, but as Garrett reached his own six-foot-four height, he estimated the military man to be closer to five eleven.

Not wishing to antagonize, he kept the smile to himself, weighing odds on single combat. If he were uninjured, this man would prove no match to Garrett's wiry agility and years at sea. A sudden sharp pain, shooting through his lungs, reminded him that his current injuries would perhaps impede victory.

"On the next tide, you will all be transported to our stronghold at USMA," Holden continued, pointing an index finger at each man in turn.

"Where?" An inmate—barely sixteen, Garrett estimated by the lack of facial hair—asked. Garrett thought of his own boys and prayed he'd never see them in such a state of malnutrition.

"West Point, or some other, closer stronghold… never mind." Holden shook his head and flapped rigid fingers. "Know this—you will be tried and sentenced."

Then, Holden shot Garrett a direct glare. "Unless we find something of value for which to retain your services."

Within the hour, wrists and ankles shackled via short chains to the men in front of and behind him, Garrett shuffled in awkward snail's pace down the hill toward the Atlantic. The ocean looked angry today, and yet he'd rather be out riding those waves than in the stink of this compound. Automatically, he scanned the horizon. Drizzle soaked them within moments, while the wind chilled to the bone. Then his heart stilled. There, amongst the three ships at anchor, floated his *Isle Sky*. Her clean lines and well-trimmed masts drew the eye. Beautiful and buoyant, stern high as though daring any man but he to take the helm.

"That's my girl," he said, focusing all his attention on the sight at hand to take his mind off the pain renewed with each step.

Expecting to be transported on one of the cargo vessels, he was astonished to find, instead, they were herded into a long boat he recognized as his own. A foreign crew manned his beautiful four-masted schooner. Who would dare sail his ship? Fury mounted to sting his cheeks and warm his blood against the bite of the weather.

What he had expected would happen, he could not articulate. To this moment, he'd only ever considered the three of them would break free. As he planned, and studied their jail, he'd fully expected that they would be broken out by his remaining crew. Ultimately, in any scenario, regaining their ship would fulfill their plan. This, in fact had consumed his every waking thought. But now...

The tug at his wrists opened a gash along the bone and focused his attention on the present.

What would he do? He scanned his ship. All seemed in good order, saving the foreign faces manning the stations. Where were his men now? He prayed they had made it to shore. Scanning the faces of the men assembled, his confidence in their escape rose.

The man-o-war two hundred yards away listed to leeward. He grinned. That last cannon shot prior to capture had found its mark.

Time was running short. They were drawing near, and his time for action—any action—ebbed away with the lapping of the current. But to the issue at hand. What could he do? He shared a look with Brian and Ruddy Roddy.

To lose *Isle Sky* when they were so close to achieving their goals bit more fiercely than the shackles at his ankles and festered greater than the slash to his calf. How could he face his men again, or be husband to Bessy? She could never respect a man who capitulated so meekly.

Dear God, Bessy. All of this so their families could be free. Released from the constant struggles of war. But what would become of his beloved wife, his boys, if he did not fulfil his duties and accomplish their shared ambitions?

Fearsome, resourceful woman that she was, his Bessy would find a way north to Cape Breton. His mind returned to their marriage contract. All these years later, he could not imagine being united to anyone but her. In fact, despite being promised to her sister, Beverly, for him, from the time they were children, it had always been Bessy. He knew she thought she came to be his bride as a second choice because of the contract, but she had been his only choice, his match. Without her strength these last years, he could not do what he had to do to secure their future.

He twisted in his seat, forcing the man on either side to mirror his action. He nodded his head, considering, while Brian watched him from beneath his bushy brows. In order to board, each had to be released in turn from their ankle shackles to scale the rope ladder and gain the deck. Scanning the decks, Garrett watched Holden stride to the poop deck and assume command.

His fingers curled into fists. Blood pounding, he forced himself to bide his time. Patience and timing would mark the difference between success and failure.

In single file, two men had started up the rope ladder before Garrett. Standing, bracing his legs for balance, he stood on the bench of the long boat and grabbed the cable bouncing against the side of the ship. In as fluid a movement as he could manage, he took a firm grip and leveraged his body to kick the oarsman full in the face. The man toppled into the ocean with a splash. The officer at the stern cried out, but Brian and Ruddy Roddy stood, shackles still affixed to one another, and lashed out, snatching the oar and striking the man across the shoulder. He too plopped into the current with barely a cry for help.

As a man accustomed to the sea and ships of all makes since he was a lad of eight, Garrett scaled the side of the ship in a matter of seconds. Hindered considerably by his hands being still bound, but not enough to sway him from the fight, especially with his most trusted colleagues following close behind, he catapulted onto the quarterdeck, slid flat to the oak boards, and spun to trip and upend the closest soldier.

Whilst the man lay prostrate, Garrett used his elbow to flatten the man's nose. Blood spewed. Chaos erupted all around.

Rounding onto his knees, Garrett scanned the area for his next mark. Lacing his fingers, using the manacles rather than fighting against them, leg muscles bunched, he launched forward and butted the next soldier in the stomach, coming up and under the man's chin, knocking him unconscious.

Grabbed from behind, Garrett bent double, allowing his weight to bring him closer to the deck. Like a springboard, he straightened and battered the back of his head against the one holding him. A grunt and a curse followed before the man's arms fell away.

Then Brian was there, landing a blow with his elbow, ending that soldier's fight for this battle.

The soldiers seemed to come out from the woodwork. Garrett's head was flung back by one, and another smashed him across the jaw. His mind blanked for a moment. The next blow caught Garrett in the stomach, and he doubled again, this time winded. A vicious kick to the groin had him down while white lights flickered in his vision.

Across the slick deck, he saw the other prisoners, including his men, pinned down.

Time flickered by as Garrett gaped like a freshly caught fish. Unable to catch his breath, he felt the pull against his shoulders as he was forcibly drawn to his feet. The sickly sweet taste of blood filled his mouth. He spit a gob in the direction of his captors.

The man cursed, his eyes bulged, and he punched him again, then back-handed him across the cheek. Garrett's head snapped back, and he felt the skin of his cheek tear. His neck creaked. Another soldier forced his elbows back while a pole was maneuvered through the gap between his arms and body, so that the irons bit against bone. It was all he could do not to fall to his knees.

Finally catching a breath, Garrett scanned the deck and noted that, like himself, the small band of prisoners had been quickly overrun and now stood as bloody as he.

"You."

The graveled voice brought Garrett's attention around.

"Shall we weigh him down and toss him overboard?" The man with Garrett's blood still gobbed to his cheek asked Holden, who strode from the poop deck to survey the ruckus.

"I should have known." The openly sweating Holden stepped closer and removed a handkerchief from his pocket and mopped his unnaturally wide brow. A wicked gleam settled in his murky, swamp-colored eyes. He shook his head. His lips moved a moment before sound emerged. "No...not yet, at least."

The soldier gripping the pole shook it viciously, and when Garrett grunted, he chortled. "What, then?"

"Strip and lash him to the main sail," Holden responded. "He has some things to talk to me about, but I fear he may need some prompting. Perhaps time in contemplation in the open air will help him gain perspective."

Chapter Four

Abrupt cannon fire caused the horse to shy and sidestep to the edge of the road. Birds erupted from the trees in a cacophony of noisy protest. Though she had known to be aware of pockets of fighting, she'd been in the saddle a long time without rest. The surprise almost caused a dozing Bessy to be unseated, but rider and horse were well used to looking after one another. Leaves and feathers floated into the rising mist of the pre-dawn. She righted herself, blinked several times to awaken, and looked around, amazed she'd managed to nod off.

Scared but determined, Bessy had ridden through the night, allowing the dun mare to guide her through the darkness, trusting the horse would keep to the dirt path. Further explosions vibrated through the air from the north. She could feel the echo of their impact rise from the ground through the animal's flanks and into her own. The horse tossed her head, and Bessy leaned across the neck, hand stroking the damp hair.

"'Tis okay, me darlin'." She scanned their surroundings while she spoke. "You're okay, Abby dear."

A more rapid volley of cannon shot, followed by rifle torrents and the screams of human suffering, prompted Bessy to dismount. Unencumbered by petticoats and excess dress cloth, her movements were free and fluid. She felt significantly lighter. The elation of not being encumbered quickly vanished with the next explosion and subsequent sounds of misery. Not wishing to be caught in the open, she coaxed Abby into the treeline and worked her way into the depths of the camouflage, seeking the cover of brush and leaves.

Reaching into her pack, she pulled out a crabapple, one of several picked randomly along the ride. Taking a bite for herself, she shivered with the sour flavor that erupted on her tastebuds. Mincing the pulp, moving it around her teeth, she rid the thickening slime from inside her mouth. Bending to the side, she spat the wad, then took another bite. Swallowing, she offered the remainder to the animal. "There, there, me lovely," she cooed softly, sure she needn't worry of being overheard in the deafening battle. "Be strong now."

As if in understanding, the horse's ears bent forward before her lips lifted from the large brown-tinged teeth, yet she didn't whinny. Then, in one bite, the mare gnashed the fruit and swallowed. Bessy smiled. "I'll walk beside you now, me darlin'," she whispered. "We go together. You and me."

Deep in the woods, the sun penetrated the canopy only in ribbons of color, reminding her of her youth in England. She'd grown up on a vast expanse of property with a hardy forest. Those were times when she struggled to make her way, find her place. Often, before the sea came calling, she would sneak to follow her brother, Brian, everywhere. It was then that she had fallen in love with his best friend, who was, at the time, betrothed to her sister.

Certainly, hers had not been the expected behavior for a daughter of a wealthy landowner. Never allowing herself to imagine Garrett had feelings for her, Bessy turned her passion to the soil and all things grown, learning everything she could about medicinal remedies. For so long that had been her only respite.

For a moment, she was able to block the fighting and fall back in time. Bessy suppressed a grin, remembering how, in her youth, she seemed to have few prospects. With a beautiful, accomplished, and promised older sister, Bessy had alternated between adoration, envy, and guilt, Beverly's marriage contract to Garrett a constant thorn that had threatened to rip her tender heart.

Garrett McGuire's family lands bordered the MacLeod holdings. Their families were often in attendance at one another's gatherings, and it had been arranged by their mothers and understood from their birth that her sister, Beverly, and Garrett would one day wed. Had she known Garrett not only returned her love but had schemed with Bevvy to alter the contract, she might have been saved so much heartache and spared her sister the same. But that was all behind them now.

Her gaze caught on the determined efforts of a bee servicing the wild flowers close to her feet. "My sweet Bevvy." Bessy sighed. It had been the sting of the bee which changed the courses of their lives. For something that had stung, the result was the change they had all needed.

In nearly losing her life to what some would consider innoxious venom, her sister determined to not take no for an answer, and as a consequence, she not only married her one love, but ensured Bessy did as well, having seen what Bessy had strived so hard to hide. Now, Beverly had a brood of children of her own to keep her constantly amused, with a gentleman husband always at the ready to amuse as well. How lucky they were in their stability on the other side of the world.

Bessy touched her lips, remembering Garrett's first kiss, and knew she wouldn't trade places with her sister. She yanked a clean kerchief from her trouser pocket and wiped both her nose and eyes. The white linen came away soiled with ash. The air, thick like powder, rained down like a mist, coating everything along the way.

"Oh, Garrett." She neatly folded, then unfolded the linen, observing the thickening haze. Her fingers shook. She choked back the sob, swallowing the sound. That he be alive was her internal chant.

"No." She addressed Abby. "He is alive. He must be."

With care, Bessy wrapped the material around her face, securing the ends behind her head, under her sloppy hat. Pulling the horse's head lower where the air seemed less dense, she tried to go below the fog of soot, alert to the close proximity of the battle grounds.

Gunfire grew ever closer. The crack of the tree bark where the lead lodged made her stomach drop, and ice filled her veins. Yet she didn't stop. She must approach to be sure this wouldn't be a housing for prisoners of this war. She spotted a deer trail and led Abby forward. Over stumps and tree roots, around boulders, through the mire, she continued, aware of the danger. More conscious than ever of what life would be like if she were unable to find and free Garrett through bribery or any other means, she nevertheless could not imagine life without him in her life.

"Every man has his price," Garrett had said on more than one occasion. "You need just discover the cost and have a willingness to pay."

Bessy had money enough, she was sure, if money be the price of his freedom. She had often chided Garrett that he had been born with the Midas touch, like his father before him. An ability to find where others dared not go. So much so, he'd gained a reputation, and that was why she feared most especially for his safety now. Perhaps too many suspected... She let the thoughts fade. There would be nothing gained by pondering where she had no facts.

A bramble caught the fabric of her coat, and when she yanked, the cloth tore. She swore under her breath. The freedom of releasing the oaths out of earshot of children gave her an unaccustomed sense of freedom.

After another hour of struggling through the brush, she came to a clearing. Easing out of the treeline, she peered first one way and then the other. She could smell the ocean above the fresh iron scent of blood. She choked back a gasp. Bodies and limbs littered the ground like debris left over from a parade.

Uncertainty gripped her. Prudence would see her hold still within the cover of the tree canopy until nightfall, or retrace her steps and find a way around. Yet she could not afford the lost time or distance. She straightened her shoulders. There could be no help for it. Bessy nodded with the decision. Reaching to the back of the saddle, she unlaced the rope. Then she stepped clear of the cover of the brush and gathered some large logs and smaller branches. Heaving, she lashed three together and woven in the branches to make a litter. Sweat trickled down her sides. Standing, she caught her breath and lifted the flop hat to wipe her brow, before pulling it back in place and stowing the kerchief in her pocket.

"Here." A man groaned. "Help me."

Leading Abby further onto the clearing, toward the injured man, Bessy's skilled healer's hands and keen eye scoped for the source of his wound. Multiple lacerations had caused his stomach to gap open. Having left home with the intent to find her husband, she hadn't foreseen the massive need of her skills if she came across wounded men. An oversight, to be sure, since she had expected to run into battle areas in her search.

With limited supplies, she was unprepared to mend, yet she couldn't walk on through the carnage, or away from her duty. Ripping the soldier's shirt to shreds, she wrapped his torso as best she could before, as careful as she could be in the circumstances, she pulled and rolled until she had the man firmly lashed to the litter.

Breathing hard, she searched the area for any signs of immediate danger and then for medical tents. Drums echoed around the clearing. Marching feet matched the staccato beats. She had to pick a side. The loyalist and British? Or the colonist? Each came with its own set of dangers for her, as she posed as a man and was not partaking in the battle for either side.

Imagining Garrett in the hands of his enemy, the loss of ship and crew weighing down on him, made her move forward. Within a few feet, she'd tourniquet a leg which wouldn't see the end of the day. Leaving him propped against a tree, she moved on. Here and there, she stopped and offered comfort for those with only moments to live and crowded her litter with two more she felt could be saved if she managed to find more medical aid.

Abby's step faltered in the substantial divots of the earth where mortars had only hours previous rained down, but with a strong tug, Bessy encouraged her on. Now at the other side of the clearing, with the next stretch of woods ahead, she noted the tents pitched to the side of a river. Nauseous scents of blood, gore, keg powder, and stewed meat clogged the air as much as the ash. All at once, the next obstacle presented itself. How to be rid of the men on the litter, make a plausible excuse, and be on her way?

Women, some with babies lashed to their backs, swarmed the encampment like ants in their mound. Wash basins hung over large fires, right next to the cook oven and the medical tent. Chaotic organization placed the displaced, tended to the wounded, and fed the hungry who could wait their turn. Bessy kept her head down and walked directly to the larger of the shelters. No one had time to spare for anyone not suffering from a battle injury.

In a few swift moves, she had unlashed the litter and allowed it to fall, knowing the men would be seen to. She prayed their lives would be saved but took no time for self-praise. There could be no such thing in times of war. Everyone did what they had to do for whichever side they chose. She scanned the surroundings. Her main occupation had to be the location of her husband.

Quickly winding the rope and replacing it at the back of her saddle, Bessy rounded the camp with the sole intent of being on her way. She aimed to make no one the wiser for her crossing the battlefield. On a tonal level all its own, a sound every mother recognized made her hair stand on end. The sounds of childbirth. The strangled moaning came from straight ahead, this side of the line of brush. She paused and searched the ground cover for the source of the noise so distinctly female.

The sun had risen above the trees, its warmth and merriment a blight on the morning's events. A groan erupted much closer, and Bessy stepped toward the sound, frustrated that she could hear but not see the source. Abby's ears perked.

"Lead me to her, dear Abby," Bessy said. "Where is she?"

All attention focused on finding the mother, the sounds of battlefield and camp fell away. Bessy stepped into the dense foliage, Abby crashing her bulk in beside her, the tether held loose in her gloved hand. Closing her eyes and concentrating, she allowed instinct to guide her. She turned her head and opened her eyes. Just to her right, she spied bared feet, the heels pushing into the soft soil, creating muddy ruts.

Bessy leaned against Abby's side and forced her to sidestep further into the woods, glancing back over her shoulder to see they were not followed. Then she tethered the horse where she could munch the sweet spring grass between saplings.

"You rest here a moment, love," she said to the horse, and patted the flank before returning to the source of the bare feet.

Bessy squatted low, again thankful for the breeks, and peered through the foliage. She had to get on her hands and knees to crawl under the bramble to get where the girl had lodged herself for presumed protection. The small opening could have been the den of a fox, for the undergrowth encircled the woman like a cave, providing shelter and seclusion.

This was no matron. The girl may have been sixteen, if she were a day, Bessy surmised. Where was her family? Damp reddish-orange hair plastered the sides of pale cheeks. Moss-green eyes widened with Bessy's intrusion into her cubby.

"'Tis all right," Bessy crooned. "I'm here to help."

The girl opened her mouth wide as though intending to scream and shook her head. Bessy pounced forward and clamped her hands across the gaping lips.

"No, no, 'tis okay," she said and reached quickly to remove her hat and lower the strip of cloth from obscuring her face. "I am a woman. 'Tis my disguise."

Feeling the ripple of a contraction tighten the firm belly so close to her thigh, Bessy removed her hand. Pain slashed the girl's features, and her eyes seemed to lose their focus. Bessy lifted her hand and held it tightly, while her fingers stroked the rounded mound of her belly. She began to breath with the girl's pants, then as they came to an end, she smiled. "And a healer."

"Why?" The girls eyes flew rapidly from Bessy's face to her garb and back again.

Bessy stroked the girl's cheek and made small moves of examination while she helped the laboring woman adjust her position. Using both hands, she cupped the rock-hard mound, trying to gauge how far along the labor had progressed. "As you know," she began conversationally, trying to encourage trust, "a woman dare not travel alone. Not in these uncertain times."

"With…the…army?"

"No," Bessy replied levelly and shook her head, deciding truthfulness would not harm her here. "My husband's been captured. I go to seek his release."

"Oh," the girl replied weakly, while another contraction overtook her.

Bessy noticed the bit of wood which had fallen to one side with its deep grooves of teeth marks. Retrieving the flask from Abby's saddlebags, she rinsed the bit and placed it between the girl's teeth. They needed to maintain the secrecy of their location.

Sweat coated the girl's face and neck despite the chill. Bessy helped her to drink. It seemed she had scurried into this spot with little thought of anything other than hiding. There was no water or provisions. Thankfully, Abby was loaded with everything she would need.

Within moments, Bessy had maneuvered the small frame onto a saddle blanket, provided a preliminary examination, laid out her supplies, and readied herself for the next contraction.

"Thank you," the girl whispered in a hoarse voice. Then her frank gaze took in Bessy's shorn head. "Will he recognize you?"

Bessy traced a palm over the cropped edges, remembering times when Garrett had seen her in much worse states and grinned. "Yes, I think so."

Pain gripped the girl's features like a hand squishing dough. Her brow pinched, and she closed her eyes. While her hands cupped the firm roundness of her belly, the full mouth thinned as she bit down on the wood. A dribble of blood seeped from the laceration to the corner of her mouth. She breathed heavily through her nose, and a muffled moan followed. Her heels dug deeper trenches.

Bessy positioned herself between the girl's legs and examined the cervix. "Is there anyone I can get for you?" she asked. She shed her jacket, laying it next to her, then rolled the sleeves of her shirt. Using the cuffs of her hands and her fingertips, she skimmed the swollen belly. Determined movement beneath the skin greeted her touch.

"No."

"What's your name?"

Bessy eased the skirt up the woman's thighs and poured water into a small dish from her medical bag.

"Carolanne Hensbee."

"That's a lovely name," Bessy returned, seeing the time for pushing coming close. "Your husband?"

"Soldier."

"Won't he worry for you?"

Carolanne's eyes flashed. "If he had a care, he'd have left me home with me ma instead of tending to him on the battle front."

Families accompanying the soldiers was a commonplace occurrence. Bessy felt this was no life for anyone, especially if the husband died. She feared what would happen to the girl if her husband died and she were left to fend for herself. Bessy shook her head to dislodge the thought. Nothing could be done about what would be. All that mattered now was seeing this woman through the birth of her child.

"Ahh…" Carolanne groaned low in her throat. Her body tensed, shoulders rounded, and knees rose to encircle her mound. "Sweet mercy, protect me."

Bessy's hands braced the inside of the woman's thighs. A furred head crowned briefly before disappearing back up the canal.

The contraction passed, and Carolanne fell back to the ground, her head rolling from side to side while tears sprang to her eyes. "Marie Ellis lost her daughter a fortnight ago. Came during a battle like this. She drowned herself in the river the next day."

"You're not Marie Ellis," Bessy said in quick retort. She reached to lift Carolanne's head from the ground, cupping her neck but ensuring their gazes met. "I can tell you are a strong woman, Carolanne Hensbee. You will see a strong child into this world. This is your duty, and you must not give up."

"Me ma told me to come along with Burt. She said it be my duty and I was obliged to do what I could to see him successfully defeat those British bastards— ahh! How. Long. Now?"

Bessy winced at the implication of which side she'd stumbled into, but knew it really didn't matter. In a few deft maneuvers, Bessy had Carolanne rolled onto her hands and knees and positioned against the trunk of the tree, with large rocks placed under the heel of each foot to allow her purchase to push. It was then that Bessy noticed that the girl hadn't come unprepared, as she'd originally thought. Further into the bramble, she had stashed a sack, presumably with food, clean cloths, and other provisions.

Bessy quickly pulled the sack toward her and rummaged through the contents. She laid a shawl on the ground between the woman's legs. "When I tell you...push. Push, Carolanne, for all you are worth. For the love of your child, push."

The girl nodded her head vigorously, peering at Bessy from under her arm where her head hung. Her wide eyes seemed to swim in her face splotched with color and awash in sweat and tears.

"Push, Carolanne. Push!"

The infant slithered into the world, and Bessy wrapped her in her mother's shawl. A lusty cry shattered the sudden quiet, and both women froze and looked around. Then they met each other's eye and laughed. Carolanne rolled onto her side, exhaustion threatening to claim her.

"Your daughter." Bessy handed the bundle to her mother, then helped her into a more comfortable pose. "'Tis best to latch her quickly."

Carolanne pulled at the bodice of her gown, fumbling with the ties one-handed. Bessy made to assist, but the girl shook her head. "'Tis okay. Don't thou fuss. I must learn."

Bessy leaned back on her haunches and rolled to sit so her backside rested on her booted heels and nodded. "I will help you to the river to clean?"

Again the girl shook her head. "I'll make my way." She stared down at her infant and then back at Bessy. "What is thy name?"

Bessy frowned. To give her name could be tantamount to discovery. Slanting her gaze to take in the full form of the girl, she shrugged. What did it matter now? The two had shared so much, she could not fear from this new mother.

Carolanne reached and stroked Bessy's forearm, her moss-green eyes as soft as the foliage surrounding them. "I'll not give thee away."

"Bessy."

"Bessy," Carolanne repeated. "I shall call my daughter Bessy to remind me what courage really is."

Chapter Five

Even moving his tongue required an extraordinary amount of effort. Still Garrett couldn't muster a lick of spit. If ever he needed one of Bessy's herbal broths, it was now.

Bessy. The thought of his passionate wife caused an additional pain in his heart and a weight on his shoulders. He had to get her and their family to safety. If he or any of his men broke, all would be lost. Not just the campaign, but their futures.

No, he couldn't consider that. He needed to focus as his wife had shown him to do. Take a mental inventory of what worked and then focus on the areas that didn't.

"The mind is the most powerful healing tool," she would often say of those who seemed to come back from the brink, compared to those who just up and died for no apparent reason. She would reach to cup his cheeks and lock her gaze with his. "You always remember that, my love. You never ever give up."

Though it had always been an unspoken pact between them that they would never discuss or acknowledge the many dangers of his work at sea, Bessy would often school him on practical advice in the event of injury. He should have told her how invaluably that knowledge had served him and his crew these many years. Why hadn't he told her with every breath how much she meant to him? How he could never imagine having had a life so full without her.

He squeezed his eyes closed until the pain of that small motion forced his muscles to relax. Even tears were an impossibility. Sweat failed to pool hours ago, and the blood had dried to a crust, holding his skin in stiff alignment to where he'd crumpled after the whipping. Humiliation burned, forcing him to straighten against the pain, biting back the groan.

Twenty lashes, with the cat-o-nine-tails doing its job to slash and maim the skin. Garrett recalled less than half, having lost consciousness with the white hot bursts of pain each stroke evoked. How he prayed he didn't soil himself or call out. While he'd know soon enough on the former, he didn't want to know the latter.

He tried to shake his head to clear his thoughts and plan, but the movement brought a heave to his gut. He braced for the bile, stomach tightening. Curbing the impulse, a gush of saliva finally pooled in his mouth and he swallowed gratefully. Eyes fused closed, he rubbed his face gingerly against the deck until he felt the skin pull and the clot release. He opened one eye to a slit to peer at his surroundings.

Getting his bearing, the sway beneath his cheek let him know they were away at sea. In what direction, and to which destination, he could only guess. Through the miasma of trauma-induced fog, Garrett forced his brain to focus nautically. Where would Holden take his ship? Garrett gnashed his teeth, the agony in his jaw increasing to dissuade his impotent rage.

Feet thumped all around him. Chatter like birds finally penetrated, and he started to focus on what they said. He wasn't surprised by the mix of dialect and accents. From French, to Spanish, and the Gaelic Irish, like most crews they spoke in a shorthand all could understand.

Coming into awareness, he noted that his hands were lashed to his feet. He lay on his side, curled around the post run red with his blood. The coppery scent mixed with that of ocean brine and stale-sweated men.

He grunted and banged his forehead against the planks. Think, he urged himself. What did he always tell his crew? "Someone always survives," he would remind them before going into particularly dangerous waters or facing down a stormy swell. "The difference between surviving and not surviving is based on the ability to keep your head and think rationally."

Now he had to take his own advice. Stop thinking of the *Isle Sky* as captained by someone else. Let go of ego. Whether all or any of his crew had been captured like he was meant nothing until he could be free to find them. They would keep their silence. Any other cargo lost could be regained. Priority, at the moment, had to be getting free.

Rolling his shoulder slightly onto the agonized blade of his back, he peered to the sky. Gunmetal gray and brimming. He sniffed. The wind freshened, and the crack of the top sails rang like cannon fire as they caught and held. The sun, filtered through the low cloud, showed they moved toward—land. How long? Hours, maybe. Would they outrun the impending storm or ride right into it?

Garrett twisted farther, ignoring the flashing pain from his back, and took stock of his ship. Under the right guide, she'd do well in even the worst conditions.

However, in an amateur's hands…

"What you lookin' at, maggot?" One of the foreign crew stooped over him, a waddle of white slime punctuating the thin-lipped sneer. "Capt'in no more. You ain't givin' orders now, is ya?"

Garrett recognized the former crewman. Stanley Dutch, beached last season for skimming rations. He'd been a filler, necessary when so many had succumbed to fever. Unlike other captains, because he both owned and operated his vessel, he could allow his men recovery. That kept them healthy and able to work, but more importantly, loyal.

All ships were a community unto themselves, and if you couldn't trust your mates, they became like the weakest link in the chain, and all would flounder. When Cookie had recovered, Dutch had been reported and saw his last pay and opportunity, deposited on the first dry piece of land they encountered. Like any disease, a clean cut and immediate removal were imperative to continued health.

"You'll get yourns," Dutch continued. "That lieutenant knows you got loot." He pointed to his misshapen ears. "I hears things. The whispers. I knows."

Garrett grunted, unable to form words in his withered mouth.

Dutch chuckled, a high-pitched manic sound grabbed away with the now gusting wind. "I tells him myself. Yes, I did." He nodded vigorously. "I told 'im how I crewed with you. See, I'd already been forgiven those past sins, 'n' now I'm back in his majesty's loving embrace."

Once a thief, always a thief. Garrett thrashed

through the registers of his memory to consider the timeline and what was known. Picked up in Aberdeen, they beached him at their first port-o-call in Maine. Three weeks, maybe. Garrett relaxed. Whatever Stanley thought he knew could do little more damage than the loss of *Isle Sky*, and perhaps serve to identify some of his men. Was Brian close by? He prayed for his friend's safety.

"He tells me when we get it, I'll get my share—"

Limited though he might be, Garrett refused to listen or be goaded further. He could do nothing at the moment save summon his strength, and he'd never do that if he was distracted and sustained more injuries. Painfully, he rolled back to curl around the whipping post.

"Why you…"

A sharp kick to the ribs released a gush of air Garrett could ill afford to lose. He felt the crack and winced, curling further in on himself to protect what he could. He'd never get his ship back if he couldn't recover. He'd need more than just his wit to succeed. He tried to imagine Bessy's healing hands taking care of him. He willed thoughts of her to carry him away.

"You…Dutch." A firm shout stopped further assault and pulled Garrett back to the miserable moment. "Back to work. Squall's brewing."

The rain would at least slake his thirst.

Chapter Six

"Will you love me forever, as I love you?" he had asked, staring deeply into her eyes, and Bessy had answered, vision blurred by tears of happiness, "I will."

The memory of their nuptials threatened to drown her in tears as much as it stole her breath. She fluttered her hand along the horse's sleek neck. The strong muscles and dogged determination to keep moving as long as needed gave Bessy strength.

Bessy's exhaustion was secondary to her mission. The longer she tarried, the more opportunity that her Garrett would be lost and the longer her children would be without parents. Left though they were in the capable, loving hands of Marie-Kelly, kin though she was, those were not her hands preparing the meal for her boys. Not her lips reminding the young Mackenzie, so much like his grandsire, to mind his manners. She knew all too well how her Malcolm could wheedle and get his own way with a mischievous grin he'd inherited from his own da. Just how many times had Garrett talked her into his escapades? Cajoled so she wouldn't worry when he'd be away a long while. Yes, he'd always known how to get around her, and her son had the very same ability. In her mind's eye, she imagined chatting away with his future bride and comparing stories.

A wry smile replaced her tears. Decisions had been

made, and she had to live with the consequences…yet that didn't stop the mother's worry. Garrett would be the first to remind her that when they made decisions, they didn't look back. "That will only slow you down, my love," he would say. "No one needs those kinds of distractions when things need doin'."

Bone weary yet determined, Bessy continued south. At times she felt like the soldiers, moving from one battle to the next. The difference for her was that she moved covertly, never sure until the last which side she'd landed on with whatever battlefield carnage she encountered. This political battle saw friend become foe and families split unnecessarily.

For her, battle lines blurred. From that first morning where she helped the fallen, she set aside her views and concentrated on moving forward. Anything preventing her from her course constituted enemy. Therefore, anyone else was deserving of help. She found she could easily gather needed intel from the wounded on both sides, and she did. In this way she plotted her way ever closer, she prayed, to her beloved Garrett.

On the journey from Boston, she contemplated going to Cape Cod, sure any seized vessel would be taken there. Only after saving the leg of a British militiaman did he confirm her original suspicion of the coastal naval base near Norfolk.

A gash, inflicted by bayonet, had trenched in his lower leg from ankle to knee. With the bone clearly visible, he thrashed with the pain. When she found him, he'd pulled his way into the very bush she navigated.

Catching her eye, he panted. "The surgeon will hack it off. And when they do, I'll be no good to no one. I've a farm and a family. I'd sooner die than go home as an added burden to my wife."

"Hush," she said and tied Abby's reins to a tree just out of sight. Scanning the surroundings, she'd stepped gingerly out of the thick foliage to tend to the wounded man.

"Are you an angel come to take me to my maker?"

It was then she realized her cap had caught on a tree branch, revealing her gender. A stupid oversight on her part. This could have cost her life, at the least her safety. She patted the top of her shorn head and fought back a hysterical belt of laughter, knowing how ragged she now looked. But the man was solemn, so she bit back the urge and studied his features. "No, I'm just a woman in search of her man, now captured."

What made her so blatant, she didn't know.

He simply nodded. "I wouldn't want my woman alone, without my protection, in these woods," he said. His voice wheezed while Bessy took her canteen and cleansed the wound. "No place for a woman. Besides, without me, she and the children have to tend to the homestead." He choked then. "What good will I be to them with only one leg? A cripple."

"Nonsense," Bessy said. "We women love our men, and not just for their labor, you know."

Why was it men could only see themselves in one light? Whole or nothing. They lacked the imagination to see themselves through adversity. Where would women be if they considered pregnancy in this manner? Washing, feeding, the constant back-tolling, the heavy weight of worry that having a family creates. For certainty, chores would cease to be done. Better a man with one leg than no man at all. Arms to wrap around you at night. Whispered words of love. A mind to share ideas. Could he not see…?

He bounced his injured leg out of her grasp, drawing her back from her contemplations. She scrambled to regain her hold.

"The pain."

She tossed him a bit of bark. "Bite this, and don't ye yell. For certain, shut your mouth before you alert the wrong sort and we both suffer a bullet." She scanned the battlefield beyond. Bodies littered, but few moved. They'd have a bit of time before the gatherers came to collect the dead and wounded.

His eyes widened, but he did as she bid.

"Do as I say, and we'll save the leg. You'll go home to your woman and spend the rest of your days happily farming your crops and annoying her with your interference."

His cheek quirked. "And raising cows."

She smiled. "And cows."

Then his features furrowed in new pain as she turned the limb this way and that, redirecting her attention. The white of the bone showed between the exposed meat. She dribbled the water one last time, seeing it as clean as she could make it in these surroundings. She reached into her saddle bag for the alcohol. She would need to prevent him from screaming when she dosed the leg to prevent infection. She'd done this more times than she liked to remember this last while.

"You're going to need to talk to me to both distract yourself and not scream."

He nodded, his Adam's apple bobbing as he sucked in his breath, swallowing a gasp. He panted through the stick in his sparse, weathered teeth. "And chickens…for eggs."

"Eggs," she echoed, threading her hooked needle. "Tell me pigs as well for bacon."

"B-big nasty sow…bu-but a go-good breeder."

"A fine farm, you have," Bessy remarked pulling the thread and casting him a quick glance and a wink. "For sure, you keep talking that way, you'll make us both hungry."

She pinched the skin beneath his knee together and drew her needle swiftly through the thick skin, finishing the mend. He moaned, and she patted his thigh. "This will hurt. Brace yourself. There's no other way."

Air erupted from his nose and she saw his jaw clench. He pinched his gaze into a slit. "Goat's milk, then, for cheese."

She drew out the bandages, wrapping the strips firmly over the bone. "Eh?"

White lips moved in the pale face. "Goat's milk for cheese."

Movements efficient, she knotted the fragments together, doing her best and praying for no infection. "Do you grow wheat for flour?"

His head sagged, and for a moment she feared he'd lost consciousness. Then his face lifted. "Bread."

"Yes, the bread will complement the breakfast. Now you've gone and made me truly hungry." Up on her haunches, she patted his cheek. "Don't give in on me now."

Dazed eyes stared back, the white reflecting back her concerned face. But finally his pupils reacted, and he spit the bark to the side as a shadow of a smile lifted his cheek. "Not I."

"I'm going to rip the fabric of your shirt. I need to bind a splint for the leg."

He sat up and allowed her access, his face nearly as gray as the sky above, save for two dark splotches, which gave her hope.

"Your name, angel?" he asked as she helped settle him against the base of a tree.

This had happened far too often on her journey. She'd helped many, and by the time she completed work with each, they'd known her to be a woman and wanted to express their gratitude, some even offering marriage. But the closer she came to her destination, the more dangerous this became.

"You'll oblige me if I decline."

He leaned his head against the trunk. "Take mine then." His breath heaved, but he seemed intent as she made to leave. "Our is McCann. The homestead is just the other side of the Kennebec River, in Maine, near Augusta but closer to the ocean. We can smell the salt air. If ever you or your man needs assistance, you will always find it with mine."

She shook her head, then winked. "You haven't made it home yet."

"I will though…thanks to you, angel." He drew his spine along the base of the tree to sit straighter. "Even if I'm not there, you tell my missus. You tell her I remember the day I first met her at the parish picnic and how she turned me down when I asked her to dance, because I smelled of pickled eggs, but I persisted the next time, and the time after, and have never eaten a pickled egg again. She'll know you to be friend and will offer you help."

Bessy stood to retrieve her hat and stogged it low

on her head, ensuring all her hair was covered. "You'll be home soon. You must truly believe that, Mister McCann."

"I will if you tell me your name. Tell me, so I will know you when next we meet and we and your man share a meal."

Laying a long, smooth, solid branch next to him to use for walking, she couldn't think of what difference it would make at this point. Her husband was already captured, and if she were too, such was the will of God. "Bessy McGuire."

He held out a hand, and when she took it, he twisted it to kiss her scraped and bruised knuckles. "'Tis my pleasure, Mistress McGuire." He smiled then, and she recognized a boyish rogue. "Where say you, your man?"

She slumped and pulled the hem of her jacket. "I don't know," she confessed. "His ship was taken. I go now to the Cape to search."

"Norfolk, mistress," he said at once. "All bounty will be taken there. He be a lucky man to have the likes of you for a woman by his side."

Chapter Seven

The rats scurried between the globs of debris covering the floor. Plentiful and seeming to multiply with each influx of prisoners, the rats fed heartily on their meager rations and, in some cases, the men themselves. Garrett shivered and pushed his injured back against the damp of the wall. As he well knew, open flesh and sores attracted the rodents and insects by the hordes.

Across the small room, four men sat ramrod straight. Clad in buckskin pants, their faces ran with the remains of war paint, blood, and battle muck. This only served to enhance their shaved pates and black mohawks hung with three feathers each.

He was in a mixed cell. Prisoners of the war were co-mingled with criminals of every ilk. Garrett's gaze took in the throng, and when his glance caught on another's stare, it took every ounce of courage for him not to look away, such was the intensity of their hatred for all. Could he be considered an enemy, and they to him, when they were all prisoners held by the same oppressive master? Garrett forced a smile to his cracked lips, and the other man's brows rose. Finally, the man's gaze lost a measure of hostility, and Garrett moved on to continue to scan the room.

Except for the very ill, the men slept sitting up. There was no room for anything else, they were so packed in. For the prisoners like him, in prime locations along the wall, they valued their real estate. Those in the middle, as well as the very sick, didn't last long. Prone to more bites from the vermin, it didn't take long for further sickness to take them.

In the time he'd been there, he witnessed how the very lucky were paroled. Letters were sent to family and soon money would exchange hands and they'd be gone. Bribes were expected, with a document signed stating they would take no further action in the war left in their wake. Garrett had not been afforded such an opportunity, and even if he had, he wouldn't have taken it, though he knew his Bessy would pay readily enough. He'd give too much away and place too many in more danger.

No, for him, this wasn't an option. Given his profitable line of work, he even doubted they would take a chance in acknowledging that they knew him at all.

Bessy. Over their years together, he seldom worried for her. So capable. He could depend on her to raise the boys, during his frequent absences, to be honorable men. A true partner to him. But behind closed doors, there was a very different woman, who stirred him to his core. Hair down and lying silkily across her pale curves, she came to his bed wanton and giving. Garrett felt himself stir and averted his thoughts.

In these uncertain times, she occupied his thoughts more and more. He needed to get her and their family to a safer place. To the safe place he and Brian had found and already purchased. He couldn't lose hope now, so close to their goals.

Time. They needed time to successfully fulfill their

obligation, only half completed, and time to traverse these obstacles in their path.

Time was wasted here, drowning in self-doubt. The pain and itch of barely healed wounds caused significant discomfort, drawing his mind in split directions. As a man used to continuous physical labor, the forced sedentariness of confinement ached his brain as well as his inactive body.

An internal rage, the same that had dogged him like a shadow since he'd been dumped in this pit, plagued him. There was no agency in giving way to this rage. The bastards could not cage his mind, he reminded himself, and struggled to turn his thoughts to more practical items.

The *Isle Sky*. Perhaps after ensuring the cargo safe, some of the crew would follow. What use, though, if they could not get on board and sail free?

The cargo.

He smiled. They would never let it fall into enemy hands while breath stirred. Each had their own portion to protect. The core of the crew had sailed together for years now, and aside from the occasional scallywag, theirs was a trusted group. He let the burden of that worry fall away.

Where was Brian now? He checked daily to ensure none of his other crew had been cast into this hell with him. Garrett opened his eyes and scanned the dimly lit hole full of bodies. Surely he'd have been recognized when they dumped him in here a few days ago. Perhaps. Moving from face to face, he searched for a recognizable face.

None.

He released the breath he hadn't realized he'd been

holding. Sweat pearled on his upper lip, and using the ragged edge of shards of his shirt, he mopped his face. He'd blocked the stench from the cell, the smell of unwashed bodies, sickness, and decay, yet the mildew of his own odor cloyed under his nose where he'd wiped his shirt. He was still here, not afflicted with fever, and therefore was on the mend. He had to stay focused. There was always an answer.

Garrett dropped his hands to his lap and leaned his head back against the wall. He must think and plan. He wouldn't be here long. He knew as soon as he was able bodied enough he would find a way, and he must have a plan for re-securing his ship. Too many depended upon him.

Chapter Eight

Could she be imagining it? Bessy scrubbed her palms against her eyes to refocus. Yes. Her eyes had not deceived. There. Across the wide river, the *Isle Sky* bobbed in the current. The ebony schooner was one of three ships anchored in the wide river. Bessy would know the slip-stream design anywhere. Custom designed by Garrett to ride high in the water and stay ahead of the wind, he'd had it built by his family's master craftsmen, known for generations for their boat-building expertise.

An extension of that line of the family had now settled in Lunenburg, Nova Scotia. Along with the MacLeods, she felt the pull to move north. Until recently, they'd been able to ply an honest trade with fishing schooners. The war had wreaked havoc with their business along with everyone else's.

"This bloody war," she muttered to herself, fists clenched, leaning against her horse for the comfort of a warm body in lonely times. "One side against the other. Too many sides to choose. English, French, American, Canadian…"

Some might refer to the three-masted frigate as her husband's one true love. But she knew better. Though she might not mind coming second to the great pull of the ocean, she knew no ship, however beautiful, stood ahead of her in Garrett's eyes. She never questioned his love of the sea. He couldn't help it. The salt current was as ingrained in him as the color of his dark blue eyes. As his wife of some fifteen years, she never stood in his way. Likewise he never interfered with her healing and her being called away to help others, and this mutual respect, she felt, made them ever closer.

The boat was so much more than a tool of his trade. Had the schooner been anything less than a masterpiece, he'd never have been as successful in that dangerous occupation of evading blockades, countering embargos, and seeing business done despite the political wiles surrounding them. Sighting the boat buoyed her hope and gave her a basis on how to mount the rescue. She'd been troubled by what she would do, once she found him, and now the *Isle Sky* offered a means.

Torchlight flickered, drawing her attention.

She'd made it, she was sure..

Cautiously, she drew closer to the water's edge. The lap of the current against the rocks offered a soothing counterpoint to the business at hand. Damp earth, foliage, and muskeg surrounded her. Their fragrances filled her nostrils and she ached to sink her hands in the dirt and find out what grew there. Then the acrid bite of gunpowder overpowered the natural scents. Her brow furrowed and her jaw clenched.

Now that she was here, her heart raced in a panic of what to do next with this new opportunity. Her mind, in a constant whirling of thought since leaving her home in Boston, suddenly blanked. So focused had she been on getting there amid the constant surveillance and vigilance of remaining unseen, she'd given little thought to what she would do when she made it all the way.

"That's a bloody big river, by God." She stroked her horse's muzzle.

Abby offered a little whinny in response, as though understanding. In the distance, an occasional shot rang out. That accounted for the drifting metallic smell, becoming as common to her as the scent of roses. She and her mare had been so inundated with such noise, the bang barely registered any longer. However, a sudden scurry not far down the bank had her squatting on her haunches, alert.

Another shot. Closer.

Had she been spotted? She skittered back to the forest's edge, taking Abby with her.

"Someone's escaped." Her fingers dug into her boot, and she pulled her knife. From the break in the trees, she scanned the river from the army base to the river's edge.

Obscured by scuttling clouds, the moon offered limited light. Still, she thought she could see the bob of something approaching. A head. Maybe. Animal or human, she couldn't be sure. Whatever it was, in this light, it had a silky shine like that of an otter, smooth and fluid.

Another blast, so close she fell to all fours. Even Abby, unable to sidle farther, whinnied, prancing on the spot.

Clutching her limited and ebbing courage, Bessy stood and grabbed the horse's harness, conscious of any jangle. Abby tossed her head from side to side before allowing Bessy to run light fingers along the soft hair on her nose. The mare snorted but stopped prancing as the two of them retreated farther into the cover of the brush.

Placing her lips close to the horse's flicking ear, Bessy uttered soothing noises without meaning. How she wished it would calm her own racing heart—

Bang.

The shot rang so close the leaves above her head fluttered down in a canopy of confetti. A split piece of bark grazed her cheek, just missing her eye. She felt the skin rip and the run of blood down her cheek.

The horse reared, and Bessy lost her grip on the harness. The front hooves kicked out before stomping back to earth, just missing her. For all they'd been through to date, Abby hadn't experienced gunfire so near. "Shush, my lovely. Shush, now, my dear."

Trembling, out of her element, she pushed the mare deeper into the foliage, resisting the urge to remount and scurry away. She made to grab the reins three times before finally getting them. Breathing deeply, she secured her hold of the harness and fastened the horse loosely to a low hanging limb, leaving Abby safe. Resigned, she made her way back to the water's edge on her hands and knees. She had to see what was going on.

Squatted on her haunches, Bessy removed her cap and used it to wipe the sweat and blood from her brow and cheeks. She couldn't think. The fabric balled between her damp palms.

Damp mud seeped into her breeks, and she lowered herself until she was flat on her belly, her face inches from the water. Staring across the divide, she waited for the next shot. The silence of the night pushed in on her. It seemed all the night creatures, like herself, were huddled in fear of the blasts.

She shook herself. She needed to be brave for Garrett's sake. She couldn't come all this way only to turn tail and run. If she were to get her man back, she couldn't do it cowering on the edge of a river. Her mind raced. She could bed down now and buy a boat tomorrow, but not without causing suspicion. Then, once she was across, how would she find Garrett in the fortifications?

Splash.

Bang.

They'd been waiting for their moment.

The shot blasted the bark off a tree not five feet away. A flurry of leaves rained down, and wakeful birds complained. Abby's prancing and neighing were lost under the cover of the sounds of disturbed nature. Perhaps she was only imagining Abby's sounds as a means to avoid the imminent danger across these murky waters.

Bessy didn't dare move. She couldn't, not without giving herself away. Even when Abby whinnied, Bessy held her position, held her breath.

Then the silkie emerged, wiggling up along the bank of the river as slick as a snake. She watched mesmerized, as he slithered, barely discernible, from the water to the muddy bank. Had she not been in her exact position, she doubted she'd have been able to see him at all. The darkness placed everything into shadows that swayed and moved as the moon went in and out between the clouds. Distinct features were impossible to identify. Sure the silhouette was male, she retrieved the knife from her boot, gripping it as Garrett had taught her, blade turned toward her, running along her forearm, ready to attack and defend her person.

From mere feet away, a moan escaped the being, like that of a wounded animal. Deep and guttural. He rolled, and his arms flung to the side. He didn't know she was there.

Across the distance of the river, Bessy heard shouted orders, but no further shots. Time lost meaning as she waited. A wheeze struggled from the silkie, for that's how she thought of the apparition as she watched. Had he been shot, or was he merely exhausted from the swim?

After what seemed like an eon, the night creatures regained confidence, and the undercurrent of chirps and hums filled the vacuum of silence which had hung so oppressively after the disturbance moments before. Abby snorted and rustled, surely bent on munching some nearby grass. The chomp of gnashing teeth seemed amplified.

The horse had been heard and identified. Quicker than she would have expected, the man rolled back on his stomach, drew up his knees, braced his arms, and lifted his head. He reminded her of a powerful panther bracing to pounce.

Bessy stiffened and dared not move even to quiet her horse's hysterics. She had avoided all such situations so far and had no inclination to engage the stranger. Not this close to her destination. Better to wait him out and see him gone. In reality, despite all of Garrett's teachings, she'd never stand a chance against an escaped soldier. If he didn't go soon, her only hope would be either to flee, chancing being caught by patrols and…she mustn't think of that…or to reason with him that she posed no threat to his escape.

The head moved side to side as though he were

trying to pick her out of the darkness where she had made herself as small as possible under the spreading branches. Was this her imagination? How would he know she was there?

Then with a whooshed, "Ha!" one of his arms folded in on itself and he lost his balance, slanting sideways. A groan announced the impact on his shoulder, and then he went quiet. Without further thought, Bessy was on her feet.

She scurried, keeping low to the ground, so as not to draw attention from across the river, and drew up a measured pace from the silhouette's head. His head rolled from side to side. The whites of his eyes reflected the little available light. Covered in muck, the silky shine had gone.

His gaze caught on her, and his eyes widened at her appearance. Staring, his gaze tracked a path from her uncovered head, across her face, and down to the knife fisted against her bent knee.

She followed the gaze and then returned her focus to his face.

He shook his head.

She stowed her knife back in its sheath.

Chapter Nine

Had they gotten away, Garrett wondered of the four natives. The event had happened so quickly, he'd had no time to consider trailing after them. He'd been mesmerized by their seeming ability to communicate without words. He had tried to track their plan and been so caught up he'd missed his chance.

"God damn it."

He slammed a fist against his thigh, tossing his head so it bounced painfully against the brick wall. Wasted opportunity. Maybe his only chance to escape. He now knew he'd inadvertently helped without realizing the implications.

Dawn was breaking, announced by the bugle and drums more than a change in the light from within the prison.

A guard had stamped to the cell door, followed by a lieutenant.

The occupants hushed and waited.

The officer squared up to the door, his head jutting forward from his stationary body. "Which one?"

The guard has his rifle unslung and gripped between his hands. He pointed with the muzzle. "The big one in the corner."

"Anyone else?"

The sentry, a youth barely able to fill the shoulders of his uniform, peered between the bars. His blotched face featured high color on his cheeks, shrouded by a bushy brown brow meant for a much older man. A nasty gash trailed from temple to jaw. Stitched in haste by inexpert fingers, Garrett guessed. His Bessy's stitches were always so fine and delicate whether on fabric or human flesh. A rare woman and a fine healer.

"Can't be sure," the young man said at last.

"But you are sure of that man?" Sausage-like fingers pointed between the iron bars, identifying Garrett.

"Yes, sir."

With a nod from the lieutenant, the guard whistled for a companion. Haltingly, he shouldered the weapon and opened the grille, leaving the other to have his musket at the ready. Striding into the cramped space, thoughtless of stepping on weak and injured prisoners, the stout guard paused for a fleeting moment in front of Garrett.

In that moment, Garrett registered fear in the boy's gaze.

Good.

Then he checked himself. The youth could no more help which side of the bars he stood on than Garrett could. He had a job to do. He had an incident to be accountable for. And at this point, everyone had picked a side and no one was winning. Degrees of losing seemed a better descriptor for this war which seemed never to end.

"On your feet," the young man growled, compensating for Garrett's recognition of his fear.

Garrett tossed a gaze between the officer and the two guards, weighing his options between bullets and bayonet. Either way he rolled the dice, he'd lose. Yes, degrees of failing.

The guard kicked his feet, and the prisoners on either side scooted marginally away. The loss of four bodies in the cell did little to improve the demand for more room. Unslinging the gun, he pointed the muzzle at Garrett's chest, like he would an index finger. "Now."

Garrett shrugged, rolled onto his knees, taking his time, and painfully got to his feet, cursing the discomfort he knew registered on his face. A brief nausea threatened as he stood and swayed. Swallowing hard, he bit back the acid lump. Knees bent at the ready, he faced the youth and sneered. "What's the hurry?"

The boy's lips thinned, and he shoved Garrett forward with the butt of the gun.

As Garrett carefully sidestepped those in the middle of the floor, the rifle's wooden butt slammed against his back and the painful gashes not yet healed. He felt the hot ribbon of blood spurt. The skirmish earlier had pulled the flesh from his collar to his ribs.

Forming a triangle around him, the soldiers marched him into the early morning light toward the square. Drizzle fell, misting across his face, leaving those parts of him with a feeling of being freshly clean. How long had he been captive? Too long, if he'd forgotten the delight of a gentle rain. No, never that long.

They stopped paces away from the whipping post. He turned a full circle. From the raised square, he could see not only the *Isle Sky* but two other vessels at anchor. Had they been there when he arrived? He couldn't be sure. Only a scant contingent watched over his beauty of the sea. Given the chance, he'd take 'er and make his way out to sea.

He shook his head. Much as he'd love to think otherwise, he'd never manage by himself from port to open water. Once away, perhaps, but the rigging could never be accomplished by a lone body, with only one sheet to the wind.

"That's right, Mr. McGuire," Lieutenant Samuel Holden said, coming out of a side sentry building. "She's bounty to the state now. No longer yours."

Garrett turned to face the man responsible for his current predicament. "Lieutenant Holden," he said with every edge of sarcasm he could muster into his tone.

"Captain," the man shot back, turning the title into a sneered afront.

"Oh, ho." Garrett nodded approvingly. "Bounty and a promotion."

"There will be bounty when I'm done with you."

Garrett swept his gaze from the post back to his tormentor. "We'll see."

"Charges, Jenkins?" Holden turned to the officer.

"According to Smith, sir, McGuire here assisted with the flight of the natives."

Holden nodded. "Yet you didn't seek to accompany the savages?"

"Savages?" Garrett queried. "Surely you don't believe that, when you place your trust in their counterparts for leading search parties."

"Trust is such a strong word, Mr. McGuire. They serve a purpose and no more." Holden folded his hands behind his back and paced back and forth. "They are employed for a service. That is all…continue if you please, Jenkins. As it occurred."

"Sergeant Burns and I were delivering evening

rations, sir—"

"Slop, which even the rats avoid," interjected Garrett. "You ought to be ashamed to serve your countrymen in such a fashion."

"Countrymen?" Holden queried. "You speak as if we're all on the same side."

"When this war ends, sides will be meaningless," Garrett snarled. "You press men from their farms and then proceed to set those land holdings aflame. You expect them to remain loyal, ha—"

"There's where you're wrong, McGuire," Holden countered, his finger close to Garrett's nose. "They knew the price. But you—you chose the crown over your fellow Americans. You are a traitor to your country. We will never again be your countrymen…" The captain drew a deep breath, lifted his chin, and turned to the guard. "Continue."

"We separated to deliver the rations more effective-like. Each taking a tank."

"Tank?" Holden asked.

"Your pardon. Cell."

"Ah."

"They've become a bit…bit…cramped of late. Sometimes making it difficult to open the door without…well…"

"Yes, yes." Holden waved a hand to encourage the young man to hurry.

Garrett looked from one to the other. The boy's nervousness had sweat rolling down his rounded cheeks to drip off his chin.

"I positioned the bucket by the door to open the gate, and once the door was opened, I bent to retrieve the food. It was then one of the reds grabbed my musket."

"Slung across your back at the time?" Holden had resumed pacing, eyes half closed, fingers laced behind his back.

"Yes, sir. That's correct, sir."

"And then…"

"It happened so fast, sir. I can't quite recall all the details. 'Twas dark, too, you see."

"Just provide what you can."

"I made to give chase, and this man here…the one who was captain of that there ship. McGuire." The boy stumbled over his words, fists balled at his sides. "He'd taken the bayonet from the rifle and held it to my throat. Told me if I moved, I'd be dead afore I hit the dirt."

"That so?" Holden seemed to muse the words, looking between Garrett and the soldier.

"Yes, sir."

"Well, then." Holden had stopped his pacing directly in front of where McGuire stood, feet spread and braced. "There's nothing left to discuss. You aided the escape of prisoners—"

An almighty blast boomed, and dirt showered all around. Garrett fell to his knees, his cuffed hands braced above his head to protect against falling debris.

"Sweet Jesus," he uttered, daring to look up. His ears were ringing. That was damned close. Were they under attack? From whom? Was there an opportunity here?

A slight-framed boy ran toward him. Behind the youth, Garrett's gaze caught in the distance the main sail of his ship frilled out, flapping, unable to catch the breeze.

Awkwardly he gained his feet. The boy was

shouting and pointing, and his boat seemed to be getting closer.

Garrett scanned the soldiers. All had hit the dirt with the sound of the blast. It offered but a moment's reprieve. Swiftly the soldiers were getting organized. He had to act fast.

"For the love of God, Garrett. On your feet and come on. We've but moments to get you out of here."

He searched the face of the person pulling on his arm. "Bessy?"

"Garrett." She tugged, urging him onward, and then snarled, her face like he'd never seen before. "Now!"

"But how?"

In a fluid motion only his wife could accomplish, she spun him, cupped his cheeks in her hands and kissed him hard on the mouth. "I'm just glad you were easy to find—now come on."

Chapter Ten

"But who—who's on my ship?"

"By God, Garrett, enough! Move," she shouted, pulling, then pushing him into action, her fingers digging into the cloth of his shredded shirt.

Her rapture at finding her husband was quickly replaced with the terror of his possible recapture. He was in no fit shape. He stumbled, a limp evident. Her quick medical mind took in his pallor, the dark circles under his eyes, the sores and cracked lips. In these fleeting moments, despite her joy at having found him, his blood-crusted face and shredded clothing gave her pause. She couldn't imagine what he'd been through these last weeks. If caught, she had no doubt they'd be sure to kill him. She could understand his bewilderment at having her there, but now was not the time. She held out her hand.

With a nod, Garrett reached out his cuffed hands and grabbed for hers as together they raced across the open parade ground amongst angry shouts and yells for reinforcements. Within strides, they turned at a small copse of trees while the first shots rang out. Bark flew so close a piece caught their joined hands. She yelped but kept moving.

Garrett's breathing seemed ragged, and she wondered if he'd developed a lung disease. In her pack, she had tried to ensure she had everything she needed, but she couldn't be sure she'd anticipated that possibility. Nearly there, she thought, as she looked back at his white face and red-rimmed eyes.

Ahead, the lines of the ship had been pulled. One of the natives stood on the poop deck watching their progress. Two soldiers littered the dock. She presumed them dead.

No time to wonder further. With the gangplank in sight just ahead, she altered her stride and pulled Garrett on, urging him forward. They'd have to jump. She prayed he'd muster enough strength to see him over the cleft.

Feet pounded behind them as she jumped onto the wobbly section of wood leading onto the deck of the ship. Garrett's knees buckled, and he fell and would have gone into the inky mass of water below had Bessy not been holding so tightly.

"No!" She huffed the words, guttural, direct from the bowels of her being. "Get up!"

He nodded and rose to his feet, while Benge Tahlonteeskee, his arm still in the sling she'd makeshifted for him in the early hours of the morning, reached for her other hand and hauled them on board.

Benge pulled the plank, and the ship edged away, not nearly as quickly as they needed.

She fell to all fours, her fingers scraping the wood, grateful she'd made it this far. Then more gunfire volleyed, splintering pieces from the thick mahogany mast. If they lost the one piece of canvas they'd been able to unfurl, they'd be lost for sure. No, she hadn't made it this far only to be caught.

"By God, I won't lose 'er twice," Garrett bellowed, gaining his feet and taking charge. His face, splotched with color, had sweat running down over his stubbled chin. From some depth of reserve, before her eyes he seemed to grow in strength and size. The shots seemed meaningless to him. Unperturbed by the sway of the deck as the ship gained water in an uneasy gait, he strode to one of the natives.

"You speak English?"

The bare-chested man, of equal height to Garrett, nodded.

Garrett turned to her and pointed back to the helm. "Bessy…" He paused, and his face softened somewhat. A wiry smile lifted his cheeks. "By God," he said shaking his head. "You're a helluva woman… Take the wheel, my dearest, and do as I say."

He didn't wait to see if she'd done his bidding. They'd always been a team, she and he, and he knew she would do as she was instructed without question. Used to his ways, she understood now was the time to listen and do her very best.

Trying not to trip over her own feet, she scrambled up from her position on the main deck to the quarterdeck, taking the rudder from one of Benge's fellow escapees. Bravery amongst the rapid fire didn't come easily. Her shoulders hunched, and she kept her head low.

He turned in a quick circle to address the other men—there were seven in total. "We're going to blow those boats outta the water." Hands still cuffed, he indicated the other two vessels now with a flurry of activity as the soldiers from the base clambered on board to give chase. "You, there—" He zeroed in on a slighter of the Iroquois men. "You climb."

An indication of his head gave the man enough

information. "Climb the main sail and watch. Bellow what you see." Garrett mimed what he wanted by cupping his palms around his mouth. "Go."

Rapid fire instructions continued, until everyone had a place. Seconds stretched like hours as Bessy's heart pounded and felt as though it would leap from her body. But within moments they were set and trusting her husband's command, and she let go of her anxiety and focused, awaiting further instructions. *Isle Sky* had been built for speed. Maneuverability, hull strength, and broadside weight made her a formidable opponent. Garrett concentrated the long guns back toward the coastline and the naval base, while the cannons, double loaded, were primed and positioned to aim at the ships still at anchor.

Bessy looked back. Almost a mile separated them from the shore now. She thought of poor Abby wandering alone in the woods and would have cried. She'd done everything she could to see that the horse would be able to make it on her own. Abby was an animal anyone with any horse sense wouldn't pass up. She nodded and brushed the stray tear away. No, Abby wouldn't be riderless for long.

"Don't give up the ship!" Garrett thundered. "No matter what. Do you hear me?"

Drawn back by the blast of her husband's voice, Bessy and her seven companions shouted as one. "Aye!"

While she steered, seeing the ship pointed to the middle of the basin, away from the military encampment, the guns blasted. Daring to glance back over her shoulder, ears ringing with the blasts, eyes watering from the smoke, decimation greeted her. With each landed shot, a portion of a hull from the other ships splintered. First one, then the other. Systematic in the ruin.

Shouts and curses cascaded above the tumult, but their small crew didn't let up. A battle cry rang up from the Iroquois and stirred her blood. Something ancient took hold, and she was exactly where she needed to be.

A bellowed order from Garrett set the slight native to work the shrouds, and soon the slap and thunder of the foresail and the fore staysail as they caught the wind, and the ship lurched, gaining speed, the wake foaming behind.

Ahead, Bessy saw a six-gun brig positioned to block the mouth.

"Garrett," she yelled, hands so tightly clenched to the wheel her knuckles gleamed white. Releasing one in order to point, she shouted. "There. Ahead! We're blocked."

"No. We. Are. Not!"

His confident step brought him to the deck in a few strides. He fairly jumped up the steps. But he didn't take the wheel from her. Instead, awkwardly gathering the spyglass, he peered at the enemy.

Closing the glass, he spared her the briefest of glances. "Take 'er broadside."

She tried to speak, but her mouth, so dry, refused to form words. She gaped, then nodded. They were moving so fast now, she feared altering the course in the slightest would beach them at the river's edge.

As though reading her mind, the chains at his wrists rattled when he patted her shoulder in the manner one may a fellow mate, not a wife. Did he know that simple motion did more to bolster her confidence than had he acknowledged her as a woman?

"'Tis a wide and forgiving river. You need not fear. If we're banked, we're finished long afore, at any rate."

She bared her teeth in an attempt at a smile.

"Good," he said, as he strode back to the main deck.

Only then did she notice, through the tatters of his clothes, the rust-stained, blood-clotted lash marks freshly opened, pearling in the seams. She locked her knees, squared her shoulders, and did as she was told. She could deal with that later. All that mattered was that he was here and they were together. She had found him.

The double-loaded cannonades commanded every available hand, apart from her own.

"Keep 'er steady," he yelled back to her. "That's right. Aim toward that outcropping there."

Then the wind changed, and the sheets slackened. For an unholy moment the *Isle Sky* floundered, losing ground. Her stomach plummeted, and she stared from Garrett to the opposing vessel.

"Yes. By God! That's right."

Was he mad? Surely.

The first cannon overshot them, and then the second splashed ahead of the bow.

Yes. He'd read the wind, she realized. Taking advantage of the wind change, he'd slowed them, taking them off tack to throw off the other's aim. Now their own cannons fired, letting loose with broadsides from both port and starboard. They raked the brig from stem to stern and took out the mainsail, rendering their opposition crippled in the water. Men jumped from the flaming vessel into the depths of the river, making for the opposite bank.

"Take 'er around, Bessy, my love. We make for open water."

As they exited the mouth, passing the floundering vessel, Garrett struck colors and addressed the other men on board. Fist clenched, face shining, eyes bright with battle. "Two ships and a brig." His voice boomed. "We have met the enemy, and they are ours!"

Chapter Eleven

Hands free of the restraints, they flew out from his sides in a stunned gesture. "You agreed to do what?" All he wanted to do was draw her to him, yet he held back. His upper body closed the small gap between them. Her fresh musk, the alluring scent unique to her, tantalized his senses, reminding him he'd been away from her for too long. They stood alone in his quarters. Battle weary, raging with emotions, he wasn't processing correctly, surely, as he seemed unable to take in all that had happened.

"What were you thinking?"

"Aside from you," she shot back.

He shook his head and braced his hands against his hair. "How in the name of all that is holy am I to take them up the St. Lawrence without capture? Especially now…" He huffed, moving his palms across his face so his fingers braced against the bridge of his nose, the festered raw skin at his wrists forgotten. "I don't even have a crew."

He spun and rounded his shoulders, easing the pain cascading across the planes of his back. Straightening to square his stance, he tried to adjust his shirt over the wounds without wincing. He didn't want her to see him like this. This was not a memory he wanted her to share. Aware suddenly of his own unwashed ripeness, he marched from the bunk to the porthole, opened it, then to the door and back again.

A flash of concern narrowed her deep green eyes as she watched him without comment. She did this often. For a woman who could, when the notion took her, yammer on and on about herbs and medicine, she had an uncanny ability to be silent for a long period and just watch. These were the moments when she mystified him most. When her intelligent mind assessed and waited for the moment.

Too true, he wanted nothing more than to bed her now and find out what occupied her thoughts much later, but the roll of the ship and the sand through the glass reminded him there was no time. Already, he knew, the enemy was mustering to pursue. What they knew he had was far too valuable to give up so easily.

Noting the cut along her cheekbone, the gaunt, pale cheeks, the already slender wrists with the bones more prominent than before, he strode toward her. When he caught her look, understanding the inner workings of her mind, he flushed and stopped. He reached a hand to rub a thumb along the gash.

"You need looking after, too."

He didn't want to imagine her journey to him.

She leaned into his touch, and he read the same question in her eyes.

A flush rose to enflame his body. He didn't want pity, particularly from his Bessy. He was the protector of the family. He—Garrett William McGuire—didn't need nor want rescuing...by his wife. He would have found a way. This pact she'd made with the natives was unreasonable. He couldn't abide by it.

He whirled on her and pointed. "Even if I get them there, how will I get back?" Pride sharpened his words.

Her chin rose a fraction, her sensuous lips thinned, while a bright spark lit in her eyes. Still she didn't speak, a sure sign of her growing rage.

This only served to anger him further. Desire, tamped down, released other emotions. Did she think for one moment this boy's disguise offered any camouflage for her gender at all? What had she been thinking, coming all this way alone, and then banding with a bunch of strange men? Just what had she had to bargain in order to have them cooperate? He couldn't think straight. Surely passage was just the beginning. His gut clenched with thoughts of other men expecting a physical payment from his wife.

"No." He turned and punched the wall. "No. Never."

He faced her, frustration, desire, jealousy comingled into a toxic brew.

As though reading his mind, arguing without words, her fists anchored to her hips, giving no ground. She challenged him in her blunt stare.

He shook his head and flapped a hand, and began to pace again. He couldn't wrap his mind around it. His Bessy had rescued him with a handful of native men. The questions bounced and recoiled, and he couldn't take hold of even one to ascertain how she'd done it without getting raped or captured. Had she? What wasn't she telling him with this continued silence? Confusion, relief, love merged, leaving him unable to focus. His legs were threatening to unman him.

"If this was all they asked, it's too small a price."

Her fingers uncoiled from their fists, and she raised them palms out. "It is. I swear it," she said, her face reflecting an understanding of his torture. "On the lives of our bairns, I swear it."

His temper simmered, then faltered, weariness taking hold. He leaned against the bunk, a hand braced on the wall to keep him upright. He'd known her all of her life. His Bessy was incapable of lying to him. If she said that was all, then that was all.

His shoulders shrugged, then slumped, his head falling forward. In truth his anger was aimed at himself for being captured and losing his ship. Truly, if he'd evaded and run to sea instead of holding close to the coast, he'd never have been caught, and Bessy wouldn't have had to leave their home and children.

Unable to face the past just yet, he pushed his fingers through the tangled mop of his long hair, matted with blood and grime. He wasn't defeated, his mind screamed. Because of her, he wasn't defeated. The immediate concern was what to do with their Iroquois guests. Then he'd worry about getting his wife safely home to their boys.

Her deep breath drew his attention. Her small chest rose under the boy's clothes, which did little to hide the woman's figure. Impatience narrowed her eyes shadowed with tiredness. She held up a palm, a common habit she had when striving to make him calm and see her point of view.

"Okay," he said, raising both a palm and his gaze. What other man had such a brave wife? One with the strength he so often took for granted.

Then her lips were on his, her arms wrapped around his neck, her body pressed to his.

"Sweet Jesus," he erupted, grabbing her upper arms and hauling her closer still. A sudden fear for her safety these past weeks racked him with a hot anger, imagining all that could have happened to her. She was his and his alone. He lips crushed against hers, his hands exploring her body, so familiar yet so missed for too long.

He pulled back and drew a ragged breath. "You've no right," he said, feeling his eyes bulge. He shook her. "And what of our boys? Have you no regard for them being parentless? Your duty is to our children! You know to leave me to mine."

Green eyes flashed, and the auburn streaks of her hair seemed to flame before his eyes. Her palms flat against his chest pushed him, hard.

He held his ground and didn't relinquish his hold of her hips.

"And your duty is to come home. What when your men arrive, battered, beaten, barely able to walk, and tell me that you've been captured? What then?"

He blinked several times. Never had he felt tears rise to the surface as they did now.

Her eyes filled, and the tears spilled over to carve a trail down the dirt and blood of her cheek. "Yes, you are husband. But you are more importantly my lover, my partner, and you needed me, so I came, no matter the cost—"

"No—"

"Yes," she said, the lines along the side of her eyes softening, while the flint of her gaze continued to penetrate. "I know what you think. Though it didn't happen, men being too busy with war and battles to worry about a scrawny woman posing as a boy." She shook her head and leaned forward so their noses nearly touched. "But I tell you this, Garrett William McGuire—had that been the cost of finding you, I would have gladly paid it."

His relief at her confirmation that she was safe and whole caused the tears he'd been holding back to spill over.

Her thumb brushed aside the moisture. "There is no cost too high. As you would come for me, I came for you."

Squeezing her to him, her hip bones giving evidence of too long without proper nourishment, he whispered, "You cut your hair."

Escaping his grip, her hand flew to the shorn locks, and her face dropped. He drew her back and kissed the uneven hair. Such glorious, thick, silky locks they had been, that would brush across her nipples in their marriage bed. Hair that would halo the pillow as he took her for his own.

"'Twill grow back, my love."

Her head remained lowered, until finally her gaze rose to greet his. "They need to get to their chief. They fight with Tecumseh."

"Who?" Her words drew him back.

"Their chief," she repeated. "He has an alliance with Tecumseh, I think."

"I know this man."

"A powerful Shawnee leader. He fights for—"

"The Canadian British forces," he completed her sentence. "Yes."

"They saved you, Garrett, because you helped them escape."

"And because you saved the life of their chief's son."

She lowered her gaze, her chin tilted to her chest and bit her lip. "I did little, really. He'd have lived either way."

He could never downplay her healing skills. "He'll live to use his arm, shoot his bow, carry game, because of you."

Her tongue dipped out to lick those sumptuous lips. If there were only time, he'd have thrown her on the bunk and reminded her of their marriage vows.

Those lips. His own tongue mirrored her movement. Emotion threatened to swamp him again. In the face of such tenacity, such bravery, he felt juvenile. "My love," he murmured softly, softening his hold, then taking her bruised, dirt-smudged, and bloodied face in his hands. "You do everything. You do it all so well and effortlessly, you leave me humbled."

Fresh tears trailed through the grime, and her breath caught. She would be his undoing, as she always had been. Her body relaxed beneath his hands. He kissed her softly then, a feather's caress. A reminder of the depth of his love.

Her mouth yielded, tentative as though they were new to one another. Had it been that long? A month away at sea, perhaps. How long had he been captive? Time had dripped through the glass unnoticed.

His hands flew along the contours of her body. The hardening of her nipples to his touch enflamed him. He growled and pulled her close.

Her arms encircled his neck, holding his face to hers. Within moments she'd pulled the remnants of his shirt over his head, her hunger now as ravenous as his own.

Loath to release his grip, he pulled back but a fraction to loosen the ties of his breeks while she did the same. Hers pooled at her feet, and nary a petticoat clad her shapely legs. The shirt hung low to her thighs. It was all too much. His desire threatened to overtake him.

Lifting her off her feet, cupping her well-rounded rump in his hands, he pulled her to him.

"Bessy," he moaned.

"Garrett," she echoed, while she wrapped her legs around his waist and locked her ankles.

His shaft found its destination, entering the warm confines of his wife with the same exaltation he felt with each and every coupling they'd shared. For him, she offered nirvana. There could never be an equal temptation.

He gripped her close and twisted to lay her across the bunk. Her head tilted, panting.

"Oh, Garrett."

"Bessy, my love."

Chapter Twelve

"How can you be sure they will be there?"

The ship swayed beneath her feet. Bessy stood beside Garrett on the quarterdeck where he'd taken up the spyglass to scan the coast. Snapping the glass closed, he walked her up to the poop deck to take over at the wheel, relieving one of the Iroquois with a nod.

Listening to his instruction, she took her position. When a moment presented, she resumed the thread of conversation before he could leave again. "It's been weeks since the capture, Garrett."

He turned to her, a broad grin lighting his face. "Because, my darling, I have you."

She pointed to her chest, her finger hovering, and searched his face for the answers that were apparently so clear to him yet completely eluded her. How could she ensure the return of the *Isle Sky* crew? She had expected that once she found Garrett, she'd return to her children and prepare for their move to Nova Scotia.

"Ah, my love." He stepped closer and laid a gentle hand on her shoulder. A bath, however thrift and fast, combined with proper bandaging, a fresh shirt, and having his ship back, had erased the haggard man she found yesterday. "You said you saw Brian before you left. He and Marie-Kelly have been keeping the boys?"

A stab of guilt sliced through her heart. She tried not to think of Malcolm and Mackenzie, named for each of their grandfathers. How she missed her boys and prayed they'd behaved...at least somewhat. "Yes." She nodded, still unclear, swallowing down the sudden lump thoughts of them evoked. "But if he made it back, Brian would not stay in Boston, for fear of being discovered."

"Yes..." Garrett scratched the stubble along his chin, the rasp in his voice audible despite the wind gusts. "But he made it home, because he'd gotten away when they tried to have us boarded on the ship, and that means Marie-Kelly will know where he can be found." He paused to shout orders across the decks to pull the sheets taut and keep to the wind.

The land lay in a purple early-morning shadow to the port side of the ship. "The lads would nay accept a post, however much was promised, on the British ships, for fear of crossing the pond and never getting back."

At her look of incomprehension, he pointed a thumb over his shoulder. "Those blockades with the French. God-damned Napoléon and the God-cursed pride of the French and the land lust of the English, the bitterness of the Americans...and us, like the natives, stuck in the middle...no home, no roots, nowhere..."

He trailed off as though lost in a private contemplation. Used to this, she waited, staring across the vast expanse of gray-blue ocean, noticing the streaks of green, a sure sign of impending storm. The swirl of cloud cover looked both heavy and damp.

"Too many ships sunk."

Bessy started when he spoke. She hadn't noticed she'd been lost in her own reverie.

"My men," he said, "like most sailors, are afeared of drowning."

Bessy's gaze turned to the growing blackness ahead and the white caps of the waves. The ship had started to toss as it keeled. She faced him and nodded, hands tight to the wheel where he'd left her to further inspect the ship. At once, she watched him climb the mizzen to scan the sea's horizon, knowing he was ensuring for himself they were not being pursued. In every direction now, the horizon only offered more expanse of water.

The wind began to gust, keeping the sails tight. They had speed on their side, and a wake frothed behind them. They'd make their destination by nightfall at this rate, provided they didn't get caught in the storm. They were not near enough to the coast for gulls, but an occasional dolphin school jumped and kept pace with the racing craft.

She smiled, lost in the imagining of an uncomplicated life below the waves. Could it really be so easy? Unlikely. There were always predators.

Of a sudden, Garrett stood beside her.

"I'd pay a farthing for your thoughts." His voice had dropped in timbre, and her pulse flamed in memory of their fierce coupling. How close she'd come to losing him! Though not spoken aloud, both knew survival after a second thrashing would be possible, but she'd never have gotten him out under his own power quickly. She wouldn't think of it—not ever again. She'd found him, and they were on their way.

She shuddered.

"Are ye cold, my Bessy? Got a chill?"

Ignoring his question, she resumed her own query. "What about American vessels?"

His hand flew into the air. "Jesus, no—"

Her look made him drop his hand and cast his eyes downward.

Then he returned his gaze to hers, a twinkle in the depths. "Excuse me…that's why a woman aboard is bad luck."

She'd heard this often enough. As she'd been aboard plenty, she scoffed. "Hardly."

He bent close to her ear. "If we were alone, woman…"

"This is not a pleasure cruise, Capt'in," she chided. "You need to stay as focused as your crew."

His breath tickled past her ear. Her heart slammed against her ribs, and her breath caught. What had they been talking about? Yes, the crew. He'd charged her with regathering the crew, getting them on board prior to taking the Iroquois men up the great river. The daunting task settled like icicles on her passions.

"I don't care who'd be chasing us, I'd have you proper."

Longing for his nearness, she leaned into him, opened her mouth to reply, but a wave struck the leeward side, and she staggered. Her knees folded, and had she not been holding to the wheel, she'd have stumbled. Despite not intending to move away from his warmth, she scampered to one side of the enormous wheel and then to the other, gripping it like a lifeline. Garrett simply swayed like a dancer, perfectly balanced as only lifelong sailors can on the sway of the deck, while he braced his palm on the small of her back until she became as steady as he.

Garrett placed both hands on her hips and waited for her to be accustomed to the new violence of the ocean toss. His warmth was welcome in the growing damp coldness. He smiled as though this were nothing and continued their disjointed conversation above the growing whine of the wind. "As you know, most have already resettled their families in Nova Scotia. They may not want to be pushed into service onboard the British vessels, but they'll not piss them off by sailing on an American ship."

"But we're American—"

"We're British citizens," he interrupted, a harsh edge to his voice. "Do I not have the lash marks from the American soldiers to prove it? I'll not be taken by the British next and risk hanging for treason." His eyes, when she glanced at him over her shoulder, burned. "This bloody war's a land grab on all sides, and I'll not bend to the political whim." He paused to stride to the side and glare aft and fore before sniffing as though to smell the enemy before they showed themselves.

He returned to her side. "I'm sorry, my darlin'," he said, running a knuckle along her cheek, eyes gentle now. He rolled his shoulders. "We're a merchant vessel taking contracts to run goods. That's all."

She nodded, understanding they were stuck in a quagmire of the middle ground. They needed to keep on their toes to navigate out of this bloody mess and get their family safely situated elsewhere. Somewhere away from the constant unrest.

A rolling blackness on the horizon consumed her thoughts as the chop of the waves settled her stomach somewhere close to her ankles. "Sweet Jesus." She echoed the words so common amongst sailors, forgetting her rules against blaspheming.

"Steady on, my girl," he yelled above the gale. "You remind me again of when we were married, and here I thought you had forgotten how to curse."

She wished she were brave enough to smile in the face of this storm. But before she had time to contemplate further, he was gone aft.

The Iroquois men scampered from deck to rigging to stern, following Garrett's orders as best they could through multiple signs.

"We'll keep ahead of the wind and straight into the crests," he had told her before leaving her to the wheel. "The *Isle Sky* will slice through them like a knife through your freshly churned butter."

Chapter Thirteen

The twenty-four hours perched on the edge of the coastline in a sheltered harbor, awaiting the return of his men, were some of the longest hours of Garrett's life. Even the time spent in a prison cell hadn't stretched his nerves this much. There he'd had wounds to nurse and only himself to worry about. At a loss, with no workable plan, there'd been nothing he could do for his family, his crew, or his ship at that point.

But now…so much had changed. How…sweet Jesus, his Bessy…he'd known her strength before, but to come all that way, for him. It was only now that he could fully process what had happened in the last few days, and for her in the last weeks.

A wave of love took hold, threatening to burst the confines of his heart and collapse his chest, the weight was so heavy. An admiration for her tenacity dared him to be a better man to earn her respect, for how could he be a man worthy of her love if he didn't give in the same measure or more than he took?

Garrett sagged against the railing with the pretense of scanning the shoreline, his knees weak with the guilt of all she had endured for him.

Was it right that a man feel so for his wife? What had she called them, partners? He nodded. Certainly, he'd never considered the descriptor previously, but now that she had voiced it, the word fit. And the answer was, of course, yes. For one to admire one's partner seemed apt and all too right.

"Your woman is strong." Benge, one of the four Iroquois he'd helped escape the prison, who in turn assisted Bessy to free him, stood beside him. The son of a chief, he held a regal bearing. "She'll do as told."

Garrett nodded, glanced at Benge, then returned his gaze to the coast. Hours ago he'd dropped Bessy there with not even a horse to speed her progress. He scratched his head and contemplated the sky. Clear. For now.

Guilt racked him. With blind obedience, she was again risking herself for his sake, this time to seek out his crew and send them back to him and the ship. Another day, maximum, and with or without his men, he'd pull anchor. He couldn't chance word spreading about his ship to those who wanted to take 'er back. Surely there were spotters and spies everywhere.

"She's proud. Would make a good Iroquois woman."

Garrett stiffened, stared a long moment at his companion, caught the crinkle on the edge of the normally serious black eyes, and relaxed. A burst of laughter threaded its way out of the barrel of his chest and emerged as a cough.

"By God, you're right about that," Garrett said and thumped Benge on the shoulder. "Yes. By God."

As men who'd been through battle together, the two relaxed in each other's company. Garrett respected these men as warriors. Their people had, at great risk to themselves, their land, to their very heritage and survival, chosen to participate and fight in this war for the good of their nation.

Garrett's fingers curled around the railing. The scarred knuckles whitened, and the fresher wounds purpled. "How…" Garrett began, unsure how to frame the question. "Why…"

Benge turned and sat, cross-legged. As though on cue, his comrades joined them, their leather-soled footfalls silent across the deck. They formed a semicircle and invited Garrett to sit as well.

Benge looked around, staring at each man with an intensity which only served to deepen his black eyes. Garrett recalled his times around the fire and settled his position. Each man seemed to mirror the depths of the stories of a people as old as the land itself. Benge's voice began with a hum, moving with the rhythmic accompaniment of the waves lapping the sides of the ship.

"They came in the night," he began, his tenor voice taking on the melodic tone of a gifted storyteller. "The drums—not Iroquois—beat to awaken the People. The wail of an inhuman presence heralded their arrival. No moon in the starless sky."

As the words flowed, Garrett found himself transported to pitch-black battleground, overcast and filled with fear, and the cry of a bagpipe. Their village lay along the mouth of the great river where it narrowed. He knew this area well as a natural crossing between the two countries. Easy enough by canoe in the summer, easier still over the ice in the winter.

"Weapons in hand, we sent our women deep into the woods with the children."

Within moments, their teepees had been destroyed by the cannons, flames with quick decimation blackening the hides. The British, their Canadian troops known as the Fencibles, whose fort had been the actual target, rose up to join the Iroquois warriors and beat the Americans back across the river. However, it was too late to save the little village.

"Flares replaced the stars and lit the night for us."

Benge continued, and Garrett assumed the "flares" of which he spoke meant the sparks and fires from the ammunition blasts.

"After, to avenge our People, we joined the gray-hair known as Cockburn to attack Ogdensburg."

Garrett had heard of this battle, where six hundred men in small boats went into American territory. To think how those men faced the odds by mounting an attack on foreign soil with guns trained upon them as they approached!

"By all that is holy," he muttered. The stories he'd heard from others and his knowledge of the bloodiness of battles melded with the storyteller's tale.

Awarded muskets and horses for their bravery in battle, the Iroquois warriors were requested to join the Fencibles stationed at Prescott. In battle after battle they served, their numbers ever reducing.

"Chief Tecumseh built a new village on the Wabash, near the Tippecanoe River." Benge focused his gaze directly on Garrett.

Garrett nodded. He knew this to be in the Michigan territory.

"The soldiers come. Over and over. They burn. We scatter. Tecumseh bring us back together," Benge said, his lips forming each word with meaning and depth. "Many times. But more braves arrive from all over, including us." Benge pointed to his fellow warriors.

"They come again to drive us out. Fire in hand.

These soldiers want only one thing—to end all Tecumseh built. To finish how he pulls the People together. But our numbers were now three to one on the white man," he said in the tone of someone who had stepped out of himself and travelled back to that moment, reliving it in the telling.

"They burned every hut, cabin, and provision on the Wabash at Prophetstown, and still they wanted more. To burn us—the People."

The words carried the force of a fist with each syllable. Garrett felt the impact as though punched. Shame, combined with a need to help, to fight, filled his gut, and he could hear the tribal drums call to him. Though friend to these people, Garrett knew none of the English or Americans were innocent in the destruction of native people's homes in their quest for more— always more—land for themselves.

The other men beat their fists against the deck, and the vibrations coursed under Garrett's skin. A fire unseen had been lit, but he felt it as physically as his breath in and out of his lungs.

"But the great Chief Tecumseh advised us of this, months earlier, and we hid all our provisions." Benge nodded. The others grunted and nodded their heads in unison. "The soldiers were not successful. We scatter. They think we run, but we form up and in the night we surround them."

Eager faces lit with the excitement of the story, knowing the outcome but wanting to hear the telling again and again.

"From behind trees, up over the ravines, we pounce. We take. We scream. We burn. We avenge."

Gooseflesh rose over Garrett's arm, and his

hairline prickled with the thoughts of all Benge didn't say. The scalping, the blood, the screams. The screech from a seabird echoed his thoughts, and he started, heart hammering, though never moving from his position in the circle.

Though they may have won the battle, Benge related how the Americans followed, and the four were caught while gathering their supplies in Prophetstown in anticipation of resettling farther north.

A quiet fell. After a time, Garrett asked, "Now you go back?"

"Now you take us back to our chief."

"Lord willing and my men return."

"Your Lord must be willing," Benge said, gaining his feet as he stood in a fluid motion of grace and agility.

Garrett rolled to his knees, then stood also and looked to the shoreline, a question creasing his forehead. He raised a hand to shield his eyes.

"There." Benge pointed.

Sure enough, the brush leading to the rock-covered beach rustled. A tall aspen tree swayed, sending birds into flight. Then, like an apparition, his best mate, Brian MacLeod, appeared, like he'd always been there, on a boulder.

"By God, it is you." The words easily carried across the calm of the water. "Yes. By God."

Then, like ants across a picnic blanket, his crew dotted the shore, waving and slapping each other on the back.

"The long boat, Benge, my lad," Garrett shouted, moving to help lower it to the water. "Then home for you."

Chapter Fourteen

Bone weary, having arrived at the city's edge at dusk, Bessy kept to the shadows. Had she imagined coming back, when she left? Of course. But it had been so far from her mission and intent that being suddenly here felt unexpected.

Arriving at their home, not to cause alarm, she knocked gently before entering.

Marie-Kelly MacLeod, Bessy's oldest friend, companion, and sister of her heart, thumped down the stairs and grabbed her fiercely. Bessy struggled to retain her footing while their clothing became wet with their mingled tears.

"May the saints preserve us! There's herself at last," Marie-Kelly sobbed. She opened her arms to step back and then embraced her again, if possible, even more firmly. At long last, holding her at arm's length, she scanned Bessy head to toe. "Where have you been? Brian left as a ghost in the mist at dawn after receiving your message."

Released from her friend's grasp, Bessy sat heavily on the three-legged stool, at the rough wooden kitchen table. She laid an elbow on the edge and cupped her cheek, fighting not to let her exhaustion consume her now that she was back and knew her children and family were safe.

Marie-Kelly moved to the stove, glancing over her

shoulder frequently as though to confirm Bessy was real, and pushed at the bedded coals, creating a warm glow as the air brought them back to life. Bending to the wood pile, she took a couple of sticks and laid them on the embers, which caught instantly. Satisfied, Marie arranged two logs crossways and watched until they too caught. Then she straightened and placed the kettle over the flame.

Turning, Marie-Kelly tsk-tsked as she bustled. "You look as though you've been through the war thee self," she said, laying her hands on her hips for a moment. "I suppose you gave all your provisions away?"

Then Marie glanced around, searchingly. Bessy sat up and looked around too, following her friend's gaze.

"Your medical bag?"

"That and Abby had to be left behind. There was no time."

Unexpectedly, fresh tears took Bessy, and she laid her face in her hands. Sobs she hadn't allowed to freedom earlier consumed her. Her poor sweet mare. Was she now in the hands of an enemy? So loyal and dear…and to be abandoned.

"'Tis okay now," Marie-Kelly whispered against her ear. "We knew there would be sacrifices."

"Abby was my boon companion these many years, through storms and struggles as I go from place to place, and to have just left her…"

"Shush, now, my dearest," Marie-Kelly crooned. "Shush now."

Bessy raised her head from her hand. The meager movement exhausted her. She set her face into the crook of her friend's shoulder. The last weeks and days piled upon her all at once, and her strength ebbed away.

"Come, my dear," her friend said. "You must rest and be ready to tell us all of your adventures when the children wake. You found their father. Our Brian too is safe. All will be well now."

Tell all. Explain to her children. Where could she possibly begin? She'd thought after all she'd been through to save Garrett that she failed him. There seemed no way she could reach the men, his crew, before the American convoys would spot the rogue *Isle Sky*.

Garrett had taken her into his arms and kissed her deeply. "Do I ask too much of you, Bessy?"

"No, Garrett. You need never ask."

"Yet I do."

She drew his face into her hands and held the roughened face, loving every crag and line. In these lines, she saw their life together. The children they'd created who thrived. Those they lost, buried, yet still alive in their hearts. Staring deeply into the dark, vivid blue eyes, she smiled. "I've loved you since I was a little girl. Since before I knew what love was..." Her voice hitched, her throat clogged with emotion. "If I leave you now, you must come back to me."

His fingers brushed the sensitive area behind her ear. "It's always been you, my beloved," he said. "And I *always* come back...for you."

As she looked back from where Garrett had left her, the ship seemed so open and vulnerable despite the shelter of the harbor. Positioned off the coast of Massachusetts, lying in wait, even within the thick, forested woods, so close to the city, she feared discovery for him every step she moved away. He'd never be able to make the dangerous journey up the coast, around Nova Scotia, and into the Saint Lawrence without the experience of his men. Though the Iroquois proved more able seamen than expected, with only four of them, they'd be unable to sustain the ship successfully through prolonged weather or further attack. It had been hard enough when they passed through what Garrett had termed a small squall. If that had been small...no, she couldn't think of it without bile rising.

Knowing she'd not be able to cross the distance as quickly as she would had she a horse, she had scurried as quickly as she could, tripping over roots and brush in her haste. At one point she stumbled and landed close to where a father and son were felling trees. Resting against a trunk, trying to keep out of sight until they left the field, she gave herself away when a large spruce crashed next to her. She screamed as the nettled branches grazed her in its wake, leaving her now threadbare clothes tattered, her scalp torn, and her face bloodied.

The son reached her first. "Da?" He called over his shoulder. "'Tis a woman."

"A woman?"

The man's booming voice thudded through Bessy's brain. She knew she ought to be frightened, but at that moment, stunned by the near miss of the giant tree, she merely sat and stared. She touched the wound. "Do not fear. The scalp bleeds much more than other wounds. I will pinch it, and it will be fine in moments."

"What are ye, woman?" The stalky man removed his woolen cap, revealing orangish hair that practically glowed in the morning light as he knelt before her. The deep-set eyes scanned her face. With shoulders seemingly as wide as he was tall, he struck her as a figure from the legends of old Scotland that she told her sons at bedtime.

"A healer." Her voice croaked. "Just a healer on her way home to her family," she said again. "I mean you no harm. I've lost my horse and medical bag."

"As well you may, in these woods." He helped her to her feet, where she realized her hat had been swept away on the branches of the fallen tree.

"What's a woman—even a healer—doing out in the middle of nowhere, dressed as a man?" The gravel of his tones revealed more concern than menace.

She straightened and prepared to speak when the son pointed, a broad grin lighting his plain features. "'Tis her, Da," he said in a voice changing with adolescence. "The angel of the battlefield people be talkin' about. 'Tis her. I know it to be so."

The father turned to the son, hands on his hips. "How can ye be so sure?"

"The eyes, Da." Still pointing his finger, he nodded. "The spikes of her hair, alive with magic, Da. Like fire, they say. A flame to guide. She matches the stories."

Magic? Bessy felt her brow furrow. "What stories?" She bit her lip and tried to keep her face impassive, the needles of pain from the scrapes helping her to focus. Her bowels gripped, concerned anyone should know she had gone for Garrett. If these farmers in the middle of nowhere knew about her, then how long before the Americans found him, and all her effort would be for naught?

The father bent at the waist to peer closer. "The

battlefield angel?"

Bessy stepped back a pace, her hand reaching for the knife in her sleeve. She didn't think she'd be able to retrieve the blade in her boot.

"They said she came as a boy in youth. Then like a faerie, with deep mossy green eyes, the golden flecks glowed and she became a woman with healing hands. Bullets and cannon couldn't penetrate her armor as she whisked the men from harm with the strength of ten men."

"As few as ten?" Bessy interjected, suddenly wanting to meet this fearsome creature, stifling a giggle at the outlandish story. Feeling the knife hilt in her palm, she relaxed, and the blade remained sheathed in her sleeve. "I'm afraid you've the wrong woman."

"Then why are ye dressed as a lad?" The father asked, nodding as he scanned her outfit. "And why are ye alone in the woods? You've the voice of a lady, not a coarse common wench or a farmer's wife."

"I thank you for your compliment," she said, vying for time, unsure how to answer. "'Tis not safe these days…for anyone, let alone female."

"True." Still he peered at her in a queer way, backing off a pace, spreading the distance. "We've caused you no harm, madam. Leave us in peace."

Old superstitions die hard, and in troubled times they flood back. The resurgence of old legends when people need something to believe in to get them through the next day would spike amongst those living remotely.

Quickly, she smiled and held her palms out. Trusting her instincts, she revealed the truth, placing her faith in her own intuition. They listened, mouths slightly agape as she told a modified version of the escapade.

"I'm but a wife and mother who came to find her man." She nodded, willing them to agree. "Like your own woman, or the many who follow their men to battle to tend to the wounded as needed."

The son recovered first. "I'll go," he volunteered, though she hadn't asked anything of him. "To help the angel of the battlefield. I'll go and get your man's crew."

The father nodded. "He's fleet of foot and will double the time…" He paused, then stepped forward so he was only inches away from Bessy and peered behind her back. "We'd offer a horse, but they've all gone. Taken by the soldiers as they pass."

She could smell the ripe odor of hard labor as he came close. "What are you doing?"

"Checking for wings."

Then he looked to his son, who had stepped behind her. "None that I can see," the lad confirmed.

The father returned his gaze to Bessy. "My boy's a braw lad. He'd be there and back afore you'd make it to the outskirts."

Bessy decided it unwise to try to set the matter to right that she wasn't of the faerie folk. They'd believe what they wanted, regardless of her protests to the contrary. She was too tired to argue and too exhausted not to accept the help she needed when it was offered as though sent by God. At last, she nodded, now very concerned about the time lost standing in the forest discussing the situation.

She glanced around the wooded area. Spotting an aspen tree, she peeled the bark skin. Seeing it was still too thick, she peeled the layers until it resembled crude paper. "Have you a fire close by?"

"Yes, ma'am."

Bessy instructed the boy, who returned with a piece of a nearly burnt stick, pleased to have completed the task as requested. Hastily she sharpened the stick to a point and scribbled the note to Brian, unsure it would last the journey without being smudged away. What choice was there? She had to chance it. She had to trust.

Three times she had the boy repeat what was written and provided directions and advice, not knowing for sure that Brian would even be there. If the boy lost the note, she had to be sure he could orally relate the urgent message. She kissed him on top of his golden head and watched as he sped through the trees like the very sprite he accused her of being.

The father encouraged her to take some of his food before she too set off in the same direction. With the new bandage on her head and her cap recovered, she couldn't imagine looking any less like an angel. All of her hope had lain with the farmer's son.

The wet of the towel on her head brought her back. Knowing he'd been successful, Bessy closed her eyes, feeling she could finally rest.

"God speed, my love."

"Pardon, my dearest?" Marie-Kelly set a hot mug of tea on the side table.

Startled, unaware she'd spoken out load, Bessy lifted her head. "What?"

Marie reached over and brushed her fingers along her temple, grazing the multitude of scratches. "Never ye mind," she said. "I've the kettle on to heat the water. A bath when ye wake, my brave, lovely sister."

Chapter Fifteen

Garrett allowed no time for pleasantries or long-winded explanations. He'd a mission to complete, a hoard of booty to relocate, then to distribute to his men, and a family to retrieve and resettle in a world he prayed would be safer for his future generations. Like his father before him, Captain Black Mack, Garrett wanted his legacy to span generations.

Brian sidled up to him on the quarterdeck where he scanned the open sea for trouble in the way of storm or fleet. Garrett didn't lower the glass. He knew what was coming. They'd been too long friends and sailing companions for anything other than blunt honesty.

Brian drew an audible breath. "What have you gotten us into?" The first mate gripped the railing. "We're heading straight into the lion's mouth. We've played both sides against the middle for a long time now and managed to not give ourselves away...but this, McGuire...this..." His friend's grip left the railing to span the horizon in a sweeping gesture.

Garrett lowered the instrument and turned to place a hand on his friend's shoulder. "I owe these men my life and that of the life of my wife—"

"Yes, but think what you've agreed—"

"There's no room for thought, only a plan and then action," Garrett said, patting the other's shoulder before turning back to the sea where the froth of the waves scuttled in their wake. "No time at all. I've thought all I'm going to on the subject. I gave ye all a choice as ye came on board. You're either in or you're out." He faced Brian again. "You agreed...so be it."

Brian wrinkled his prominent nose, spidery with veins from years of heavy ale. He pulled his pierced lobe, a sure sign of contemplative thought, then glanced over his shoulder. No one had come close while they talked. "We agreed because you're our captain and we follow where you lead. But these heathen savages—"

Garrett raised a palm to silence the tirade. "No," he said. "They are warriors. They fight for their families, like we fight for ours."

"But our plan..."

"Stays," Garrett said. "Delayed maybe, but intact."

"And if we're captured?"

Garrett rotated his shoulders, the wounds still fresh enough to cause constant pain. He thanked the good Lord above Bessy had been able to tend him prior to departing. The salve offered much relief. "Then I'm dead and you carry on as captain, MacLeod. As planned. As always. You take Marie-Kelly, Bessy, and the children to the place we named Steep Creek and ensure they're settled."

Brian made to interrupt, but Garrett shook his head.

"No matter what they think I know, or where I can lead them. After this, either side takes me, they'll not leave me alive a second time." His voice grated, his words intense. The truth, he found, didn't frighten him as much as it might have, had he not so recently shared time with his wife. "Your sister knows it too. She's stronger..."

Stronger than he could have ever imagined, and

he'd already known her to be a formidable woman. He trailed, momentarily lost in contemplation about the depths of the lady he'd been married to all these years, yet he felt like he was meeting a new woman in her place. Tougher, more capable, cunning, and strategic, more than ever his match in every way.

He brushed a palm along his jaw and coughed. There was no room for sentimentality on board the *Isle Sky*. Not when they had a mission at hand. Garrett would see these Iroquois back to their leader intact, as promised. As he had pledged not just to them but to his wife.

"Take us north of Anticosti Island to the mouth of the river, the Gulf of St. Lawrence. We'll round Sept-Îles on the turning of the tide," he said, straightening to his full height and squaring his shoulders painfully. "We'll fly under British flag to the inlet to Saguenay, where our friends..." He paused to emphasize the word. "Our *friends* will reconnect with their tribe."

"Aye, Capt'in."

Chapter Sixteen

Bessy wrapped a loose scarf around her head, masking a headful of short tight curls. Then she scooped up her cape to go to the market. Having had a sister, Beverly, considered the great belle of the county, Bessy, by comparison, had learned early not to put such great stock in her appearance. However, the shorn locks continued to come as a surprise, especially now where there were so many looking glasses. At least when she was on the trail, she had resolved herself to the disguise. Her sons, by contrast, were quite shocked. Quickly though, they, as all children do, recovered and went about their business, not paying her much mind.

Unease pervaded her thoughts, taking away her joy of being reunited with her children and Marie-Kelly's girls. She constantly worried. Had Garrett been able to fulfill his obligation to the Iroquois? For all she knew, he could be... No, she wouldn't consider it. As they planned, he'd return in a month to retrieve her and the children.

For those crew who hadn't already relocated their families to Nova Scotia, like Brian and Marie-Kelly, they'd be fetched at the same time, and together they'd start fresh, away from the unrest and constant struggle. It wouldn't be the first time either of them had started fresh.

"But by the Lord Jesus, let it be the last." She

crossed herself.

Though she never would previously have considered herself paranoid, whether from fatigue or anxiety for the future, she imagined eyes following her no matter where she went. In the market, supplies were scarce and the haggling harsh, and after an hour, her basket wasn't close to full. Still she couldn't shake the sensation and made to return home.

Then the butcher Burns turned his back on her, choosing to offer the fresh cut to someone who entered his stall after her. By the time he'd focused on Bessy, his pock-marked face pinched and his level eyebrow drew low, as though she smelled bad. She asked after his wife and children, knowing his eldest to be newly married, but the snout-like nose flared before he barked the price for a haunch of beef with more bone than meat. He refused to make conversation and looked all around her person, rather than meet her eyes, and when someone else came in behind, he transitioned his focus.

Bessy tried to bargain for better. She tried to draw his attention to see what had caused a man who'd known her for years—someone whose children she had helped deliver—to treat her with such disdain, but it was no use, and she found she was losing both energy and patience.

In the end, he folded his hands across the blood-stained apron and shook his head. "That's the price," he said. "Take it or go elsewhere, Mistress McGuire."

Bessy peered more closely at the butcher. There was fear beneath his bravado. He constantly made to look elsewhere, checking the entrance and those who moved past.

For the sake of their shared family connection, she

couldn't help one more try. "Mr. Burns," she said, knitting her fingers together along the top of her basket, which hung in the crook of her arm. "Have I or mine, in some way offended you?"

His face waxed slightly and color dotted the pocks of his cheeks. "I need no trouble in my shop," he hissed, beady eyes scanning the crowd of the market beyond his stall. "I run an honest business, and you..." He unhinged his arms to flap his hand. "Either pay the price and be glad I sell to you at all, or go elsewhere."

Taken aback, unwilling to draw further attention when another patron approached the counter, Bessy passed over the coins. With the root vegetables already purchased, they'd have a hearty stew. That would surely last a couple of days.

Whispers seemed to follow her departure. What could they know? She'd barely spoken to anyone since her return. She sped her pace on her steps to home.

"Thanks be to the Almighty, she's home," Marie-Kelly cried when Bessy unhooked the kitchen door. Approaching with a harassed step, Marie-Kelly grabbed up the basket and set it down on the thick wooden counter.

The kitchen was a mess. Crockery littered the tabletop, and a sack of flour lay upright, its dust a trampled carpet on the floor. The pantry door stood ajar, and she noted other sacks, normally neatly arranged by the ever meticulous Marie-Kelly, strewn haphazardly. The thick smell of bacon and biscuits made her stomach growl.

Bessy opened her mouth to inquire and relate the reception, or lack thereof, at the market, when Marie-Kelly turned and screeched her youngest son's name,

"Malcolm," she yelled from the bottom of the stairs. "Go now and fetch yer brother. Tell him yer ma's returned."

"What's all this?" Bessy had her hands on the clasp of her cloak. "What's happened?"

"By all the saints. They think yer a spy."

"A spy?"

Malcolm landed with a thud at the bottom of the stairs. "Mama," he said, giving her a hug. His embrace strong and needy, filled with a fear she felt in the tremble of his embrace. At ten he was almost as big as she, so that the top of his head came level with her nose. Certainly he had his father's wide shoulders and would likely follow like his brother did in the McGuire height. "You're safe."

"Of course, I'm safe," she said, taking his face in her hands, her heart breaking at the concern in his deep green eyes. They stood almost level, matching eye color, his full of concern. "I told you, I had to go to see your pa, but I'm home—"

"They're coming for ye, Mama." His eyes sparkled with a pool of unshed tears, while he tried, she knew, to remain brave.

"What?" Bessy's stomach heaved, and the biscuits and eggs from breakfast threatened to reappear.

"Go," Marie-Kelly touched Malcolm's shoulder, then turned him around and patted his behind to steer him out of the room. "Like I told ye," she called after. "Quick as a whip. Fetch yer brother. Keep to the shadows. Don't let a soul see ye."

"What?" Bessy held onto Malcolm's shoulder. "No. Wait. Tell me."

He stopped and turned back to his mother.

"No." Marie-Kelly commanded in a voice unfamiliar to Bessy. "He's got to go. The girls are here and packing supplies. We need Mackenzie home."

She shooed Malcolm out the door, then turned to Bessy and took her face in her palms. "We have to go."

Bessy gaped. She'd been gone only a couple of hours. Surely they had more time. They had expected and been planning to depart, but not in such a frenzy.

"What?" She gasped as Marie-Kelly physically turned her and ushered her up the stairs. "Is he—what are you talking about? How could you know? How did... So fast—"

"Soldiers are looking for ye," Marie-Kelly said on a grunt, pushing Bessy gently ahead of her.

"What soldiers?" Bessy's mind reeled. British? American? Scrimmages between the two forces were ongoing, and battles raged not far from the town's boundary. Certainly her recent escapades put her in the path of both, but they didn't know who she was or where she lived...did they?

A blackness threatened to consume her, and she swayed just a little on the last stair, stumbling into her rooms. She hadn't been as careful as she ought to have been. Too many people knew. The farmer and his son had proved that.

"What does it matter?" Marie-Kelly wailed. "By all the saints, they searched the place looking for ye while ye were at the marketplace. Marched right in, they did, bold as you please, as though they owned the place. They know what you did. They were anything but quiet, let me tell you."

Bessy covered her mouth with her hands. Bedclothes and their few belongings lay strewn in heaps. Furniture turned over. That was why the flour marred the floor below. Bessy had mistakenly thought Marie-Kelly had accidentally spilled the contents in her whirl of cooking, this last day.

"Thanks be to Jesus, ye weren't here," she said, hands busy packing bags. "I'd never been able to hide you, in your state. You're marked for yer hair and being a healer. Yer Mackenzie, as tall and fierce as his da, told them to get the hell out, that you've been away tending the sick."

"Where's he now?" Bessy croaked, reclaiming her structured mind and joining Marie-Kelly in packing the essentials. "They'll surely come back. You are so right, Marie-Kelly. We've no time at all."

"'Tis true, they will," her sister-in-law agreed, head nodding, hands in a flurry of motion. "Soon as they were around the corner, Mackenzie shouted at me to gather our things, we'd have to be off within an hour, no more. He'd fetch you, and I was to go with Malcolm and the girls regardless of your return. We'd meet at the river's bend to the north, by the tree with the carved face where we've picnicked. He'd not come without ye."

Marie-Kelly stood to wipe the sweat from her brow with her apron. "By the saints, may the Lord forgive my language today. That boy's a man, to be sure, and a seed direct from his sire, make no mistake."

Bessy's hands shook. Now both her boys were gone, and she helpless to protect them. If Mack would not come without her, and he couldn't find her because she obviously was no longer at the market, and now Malcolm too...her heart thudded an unsynchronized tattoo.

"I can't go without them…"

Marie-Kelly tossed a bag across her shoulder, and Bessy followed suit, her own sack filled with the bare essentials she felt she'd need for the family on the move, but yet practical enough to carry and not weigh or slow them down. Finished, with one last look around, they dashed down the stairs and took to the kitchen.

Marie-Kelly's girls were already there, dressed for a long journey by foot, with sturdy shoes upon their feet and dresses that wouldn't encumber their movements. They had sacks draped diagonally across their backs, and they were just tying each other's scarves.

"Oh, my dears," Bessy said and kissed each of their cheeks. "Well done."

Bessy moved the butcher block, then the rope carpet underneath. Scratching with the toe of her boot, she loosened the stone.

"Help me here, Marie-Kelly."

Marie-Kelly brought a dull knife and they pried at the stone until they could claw with their fingers and raise the heavy piece of flooring. "Bring me the flour sack."

Marie-Kelly complied and Bessy tunneled the coin sack into the depth of the flour, and shook it to ensure no clinking. She retrieved another bag from the floor and stood. "Put this in your secret pocket." Then she turned to the girls. "One for each of you."

"Are ye sure?" Marie-Kelly's brow pinched.

"Of course," Bessy said returning to the hidden safe in the floor. "Be quick now. Distribute the food as we need it. Six people, each with a parcel. We'll move faster."

"Oh, my dear, me ma!" Marie-Kelly wrung her hands around her apron. "I can't leave her."

Bessy pulled three more sacks from the secret hole and felt around to ensure she hadn't missed anything. She had no time to think of anything else. "Then she has to come. Go and fetch her."

Bessy shook her head, there was nothing for it. They had to go, and they couldn't leave old Esther to fend for herself, abandoned. None of them could live with that, despite how hard the sour old woman was to live with.

With great care, as the door slammed, Bessy replaced the stone, packed dirt along the grooves and stood to inspect her work. The thunder of horses' hooves made her stop and listen, heart hammering. Only when the street returned to the normal sounds of the community did she resume her task. Satisfied, she re-laid the corded rug and hauled the butcher block table on top. Her shirt clung to her back, damp with perspiration.

All around her the walls seemed to be closing in. They had started to build a life here before the war. Now what? Was she up to the task of starting again?

The bang of the kitchen door caused Bessy to trip over the folds of her skirt and she tumbled backward to land heavily on her haunches. The girls cried out. Had the soldiers doubled back?

"Oh, Ma," Mack cried, coming to her aid. Malcolm stood by his side, helping her with a hand under her arm.

She hugged them close, breathing in their scent. "Thank God."

Without being told, each of the boys threw a sack

over his shoulder, and Mack reached for the stuffed leather food bag.

"First, this," Bessy said, handing him a coin sack. "One for each of you. Hide it well. Ensure no clinking. If we're separated for some reason, you know where to go."

They nodded and said in unison, "We do."

"Your cousins are your priority, no matter what," Bessy said pointing to the girls, who stood quiet, hand in hand, with eyes as large as saucers. "You are so much younger than we are, and swifter. You must never look back. You must run, the four of you, and find your fathers."

They nodded and swallowed hard, their Adam's apples bobbing in time. Mackenzie licked his lips and moved to the girls. Malcolm followed.

They had just finished hiding the money on their persons when Marie-Kelly arrived with her mother in tow. Bessy smiled as best she could while the old woman scowled and tsked, nodding at each pile of debris and shaking her head. She'd never been so happy as to not have such a woman shadowing her and loved Marie-Kelly all the more for her patience with Esther.

"Where will we go?" Esther asked, the missing front teeth adding an s-sound to every syllable. "We've no horses, and the town's lousy with soldiers."

Bessy pondered for a fraction of a second, casting her gaze between the old woman and her sons. "Mack had it right. We need to head north first, and then to the second rendezvous as planned, on the coast."

She prayed that when Garrett sent a man to find her here, after what she hoped was a safe return from the native village, that he'd recall her mention of the

McCann farm they'd spoken about as a last resort, just before she left him.

Garrett hadn't liked the idea, having never met the man, and all soldiers to him were now enemies. She'd shaken her head and explained it would not likely come to that anyway, but since the farm lay along the route north, it was as likely an alternative of last resort as any other.

She hadn't expected it to come to this, indeed, nor so quickly. Bessy straightened her features into a smile. She couldn't let them know how scared she was. So many dominos. So many things that could go wrong. She had to focus on what she could control, and that was getting them out of Boston without capture.

Mackenzie smiled down on her. He'd grown even taller in her absence. With tentative fingers, he touched her shoulder as though scared she'd disappear. "First to the picnic tree. We'll plan on the way."

Chapter Seventeen

"What do you mean, they're gone?" Garrett cursed, pacing from one end to the other of his cabin. "We can't wait here long, Brian. We might as well fly a flag and send up flares, by the deuce."

"Vanished," Brian said, lifting his cap to scratch the mess of hair underneath. Worry anchored his eyes, pulling at the edges, dragging them down with a frown. "Bessy and the boys. Marie-Kelly and our brood. Hell, even the old woman is gone."

Brian's association with Garrett was too close for him to risk entering the town, so they'd sent one of the crew, Tiller, who approached a trusted friend. "No word on Marie-Kelly. I didn't expect there would be, but Jacob said Bessy'd been labeled a spy."

"A spy?" Garrett flared, halting his frantic step to stare at Brian. "A spy to whom?"

Brian held up a palm. "Some said American, others said British." He gestured one way, then the other. "A wanted woman."

"Well, which one, by God?" he roared. "Either? Both? Doesn't matter. It's us they want. Me, especially. By Christ if she hadn't come for me—"

"You'd likely be dead," Brian said in a flat tone. "You know it, and I know it. My sister's as strong as they come. Marie-Kelly's a force. Now we need to think—where would they go?"

Brian's voice was edged with a harsh tone of flint and steel, and Garrett had to remind himself his friend was just as panicked as he and had just as much to lose.

"Men are being pressed into service on both sides," Brian continued. "Families disrupted. Young boys disappearing, and no one knowing where half their loved ones are."

"Like us."

Brian huffed. "Like us," he agreed, then shook his head and scratched his chin.

"What is it?"

Brian shook his head. "Somehow, authorities were alerted that she'd aided in your escape and helped heathens go free."

"How? Doesn't matter…" He caught a look in Brian's eye. "What?"

"There's a rumor of an Angel of the Battlefield," he said with a shake of his head. "Apparently, men are saying that when you need her, she appears on the battleground to help the wounded. That she saves limbs and rescues babies. Jacob said she'd been collecting information in exchange for healing."

"She'd never hold back her help."

"But she'd been asking questions."

"Of course," Garrett confirmed. "How else would she have known where I was being held prisoner?"

"They're afraid of what else she found out."

"She was just helping the wounded. You know how she is."

"We know that. But that's not what people are saying, Garrett. 'Tis strange times, you know."

Garrett nodded and made for the porthole. He needed air, but he didn't want to answer questions from his crew until he had time to think. Where would she go? He had to clear his mind. When they first recovered his ship, everything was so foggy, mixed with pain and recovery and the need to escape and outmaneuver. Then his main priority was to get his crew, see her safely off, and the Iroquois back as promised. She'd never put the children in danger, whatever she did.

Pacing, he returned to the porthole and opened the small window and breathed deeply. Now that they'd recovered the treasure, the men were antsy to be away. They gave little thought or concern for the handful of families not yet across the border.

"They're too many," Garrett said thinking of the four children and three women. "In that kind of gaggle they'd not go far without drawing attention."

"Too true," Brian agreed. "Getting the old woman into motion would be a feat worthy of Atlas."

"They'll go north, for sure," Garrett mused, fingers drumming against the wood paneling. Had she said something? Had she mentioned anyone? "Our women will go where they know we'll look."

Brian replaced his cap and stared at Garrett. "Someplace known. She wants to be found. They both knew we'd be here."

"How long since they left?"

"A week, maybe less," Brian said. "Could be just a couple of days. Christ Jesus, we don't know."

Garrett opened his trunk and retrieved a journal and maps. He cleared the table with the back of his hand, heedless of the mess. Then he spread the thin paper across the expanse. Stabbing a finger on the outskirts of Boston, he said, "We start where they started, and we work north to all points familiar."

"No horses, four children, and an old bitch who's as tough as a tree trunk."

Garrett couldn't suppress a grin, thinking of Esther. He wouldn't want that task. Resuming his focus, he said, "They'll keep to the forest, where they can hide." Garrett knelt on the floor, palms spread on the paper, peering close as though to see their miniature figures making their way along the markings of the map.

"Latest rumblings of battle, here, here, and here." Brian pointed.

"They won't stray that far from the coast."

"And they'll make for somewhere known. But who do they know? No one that I can think of. The MacLeod is in Cape Breton, and there's no way they'd expect to make it all that way without us."

"To someone they can trust." Garrett paused to scratch his head, his mind whirling. "Someone she can trust."

His finger paused on the map. "What did you say about the Angel of the Battlefield and limbs?"

"How she saved men from amputation."

"One man, for sure." Garrett jumped to his feet. His memory faltered, then settled on the story she'd told of the leg and the breakfast. "McCann's farm."

Chapter Eighteen

Bessy gazed lovingly at her sons. While Mackenzie carried a sleeping child on his back, Malcolm carried the extra luggage across his youthful broadening shoulders.

The longer they walked, the more avidly she had to bury her fright. My God, what would happen to them, she couldn't contemplate. One foot in front of the other, as quiet as they could, was all she could focus on. This was a hostile country right now. No one trusted anyone who appeared to be on their side, let alone a bunch of strangers whose political allegiance, and intentions, would seem questionable and scattered.

Little had been said while they escaped the city. Such a flurry of excited terror clamped their jaws. By the time they arrived at the picnic tree, exhaustion overtook the youngest, six-year-old Trina, who flopped down in the deep grass, asleep before finishing the meager snack, toppling the jar of milk.

"What a waste," Marie-Kelly tsked, retrieving the spilled container. She peered inside to see how much had been salvaged. "We only managed to bring the one bottle, too."

"'Tis fine," Bessy soothed, running a hand along her friend's bonnet. "Look at that face. She's fair done in."

Marie-Kelly's gaze softened, and the lines around

her mouth relaxed as she gazed at her youngest. "She is that."

Esther's dour face resembled crumpled parchment, yet she hadn't complained. She held ten-year-old Maggie close where they huddled by the base of the large oak. Finished with her portion of the milk, the girl rested her face against Esther's fallen breast, while the grandmother stroked the tight russet-brown curls. With each caress, Maggie's eyes drooped farther, and even while Bessy looked on, she'd fallen asleep.

Bessy beckoned to her older boy and drew Marie-Kelly with her into the deepening shadow of the willow trees. "We'll find shelter in the grove here tonight," she said, not asking but assuming agreement. "Mackenzie, take Malcolm and find small brush we can use for cover."

Focused first on Marie-Kelly and then Mackenzie, she waited for their assent before continuing. "A good bed of leaves, well within the treeline, and then we'll lean small boughs against the brush for further concealment."

"I wish we'd made it farther, but I just don't see how we can go on in the dark," said Marie-Kelly.

"There's a few willows just over there." Malcolm had joined them and pointed into the growing shadows, keeping his unsteady teenage voice to a whisper. "The boughs dip low, Ma," he said, nodding his head, the spark of adventure lighting the amber within the green of his deep-set eyes. "We should move away from the water's edge, though. That way if soldiers or anyone comes by, it's unlikely they'll see us right off. They'll be more interested in drink and rest."

"Good point." Bessy's hand reached up to touch

her son's shoulder, then stroke a loose strand of hair peeking below his cap. "You and Mack scout around and find us something. There'll be no fire for cooking or warmth, so we'll need to protect the youngsters against the wind or rain. The more rest they get tonight, the better we'll be for tomorrow."

He tapped her hand, then turned to beckon his brother.

"They're good lads," Marie-Kelly said, watching them go. "But where will we go from here? Do you even know the way to the McCann farm? We don't know these people, Bessy. How can you know we can trust them?"

She didn't, really. But her gut and the guiding strength of her soul told her they could trust the man whose leg she had saved. Unless you've been there, shared that kind of intimate moment with someone sure they were in danger of life or limb and had nothing to lose, you couldn't understand. Bessy recalled McCann's face. His description of his farm, his wife, their children. He would never have told her how to get his wife to trust her if he didn't intend this as truth. He'd wanted to be sure she understood where he lived, because he seemed to know she'd be in need of protecting.

"I know," Bessy said, taking her friend's face in her hands. "I know, and Garrett does too, and that's all we have right now. By now, he and Brian, or likely one or two of the men, have gone to Boston and found us gone. Now they'll be looking, and we need to go where they will find us, if ever we're to make it to the MacLeod."

Too true, this was a different route than the one

Bessy had taken when she set off to find Garrett in the prison camp. Their going was significantly slower without horses and encumbered by their number, and she had to rely on memory alone. She hadn't thought to bring a map. She often set out based on directions from those in need and nothing more. She knew the territory to a certain point, and then she'd have to rely upon instinct for the rest. Other than the occasional foray as a family farther north or on Garrett's ship, she wasn't well traveled.

Closing her eyes, she leaned her forehead against her friend's and tried to draw from memory some of the maps Garrett had shown her while teaching her direction and compass, but those were mostly nautical and of little help at the moment. Marie-Kelly had been speaking in hushed tones, but lost in her own contemplations, Bessy hadn't been paying attention.

"A damned miracle you found him," Marie-Kelly murmured, her head moving against her own. "Was it witchcraft?"

"What?" Bessy straightened and released her friend, hands dropping to her sides.

Marie-Kelly's cheeks blushed, but her wide eyes rounded. "I didn't tell ye afore…" She dropped her gaze to their booted feet, where she nudged the dirt here and there.

"Tell me what?" Bessy drew off her own bonnet and brushed her fingers through the thick mass of short curling hair. "Out with it."

"Word of a healing woman drifted back to the market, whilst you were still gone," she began, still staring at the ground, her hands clasped at her waist. "Angel of the Battlefield they called ye. 'Twas a comfort, you see, for as I knew, it was you."

Bessy took hold of Marie-Kelly's upper arm and squeezed gently. She had wondered why everyone reacted as they had. War always brought superstition.

"Menfolk saying how an apparition walked through the bullets and cannon to drag a man from the battlegrounds. No way someone as feeble as a woman could have done that without using magic. The size of a sprite, they said, and you know you are a tiny, wee thing."

"Really, Marie-Kelly," Bessy said, on the verge of a laugh, conscious to keep her voice barely audible. "You know better than that."

"But you did, though, didn't you?" Her gaze met Bessy's, searching.

Bessy's free hand shot out in a wide arc. "Did what?"

"Pull wounded men from battle. Fix their ails and set them straight, mended and as though they'd never been hurt at all."

"Nonsense. Those men will feel their aches and pains for the rest of their lives, mark me. I dragged those I could with the aid of the horse," she replied with a huff. "If only we had good ol' Abby here now. Still, she was but one animal, and we need at least three."

"What?" Marie-Kelly asked, when Bessy didn't continue.

"Abby."

"Yes, the horse." Marie-Kelly nodded. "What about her?"

"The farm." Bessy felt a shock wave of excitement flow through her tired limbs. "It's north. In Maine. I remember how to get there. The McCann farm is in

Maine."

Just then Malcolm strolled back to within hearing. "Where in Maine?"

"Up the coast," Bessy said. "Just beyond where your father purchased the two mares."

Malcolm's face lit. "Roger's? You think Da will know to go there?"

"He'll know we'll not go south." She clasped her hands to her waist. " I told him about the McCanns and their offer to help us if ever we're in need. He'll remember."

"If you told him, Ma, he'll remember," he said with a broadening grin. "Those McGuires, Da always says, have to listen to their women. How else would that ol' pirate grand-da of mine have found his loot?"

Bessy felt her cheeks warm. They never discussed openly where the family's financial windfall had stemmed, though broad-whispered legend spoke of the great captain who'd discovered a trove of wealth, along with a bride, before returning home to lay down his roots and establish the family in a gentlemanly fashion.

"Do you think, Ma?" he asked again. "Do you think Da will know to go to McCann's farm?"

"Whether he does or he doesn't, it's a start—a destination." She put a brave face of certainty on. "We'll figure the rest out later."

Chapter Nineteen

The only thing Bessy recalled of getting to Roger's farm was to stick fairly close to the coastline. Located in Maine where the Atlantic stretched wide and endless, the trees of the orchard bent under the constant forces of nature, yet they bore rich, flavorful fruit. If she could find her way there, McCann's would not be much farther. From the orchard of the horse farm, the shores of Nova Scotia could be seen on a clear day. She'd send the boys ahead when they got there and ask for directions. Yes, if she could remember how to get to the farm of the horse breeder, they'd get to McCann.

Thinking of the lush orchards, Bessy could almost taste the fruit, and her mouth watered. She swiped fingers across her chapped lips and squinted her eyes. Not recognizing landmarks, she cursed herself for the folly of not paying more attention the last time she and Garrett went north by land instead of by sea. At the time, wanting to be alone, they traveled by horse, enjoying the countryside and each other. Perhaps they'd spent too much time on the enjoying of each other, for now one rock wall resembled the other and she couldn't recall the proper sequence of roads and turns.

Still, it had been summer when they'd been there, the leaves in full bloom. Before the war. When the world made sense.

Now, well into fall and edging to winter, the tree

limbs were almost stripped of their foliage. Her little band of travelers were all bone-weary, tired and hungry, and she wondered if she were leading her family in circles. Everywhere they went they witnessed people and property ravaged by the scourge of war or anticipation of battle. Family members lost. Only the wounded returned.

To make matters worse, the weather turned, and the small band found themselves shrouded by thick fog. Even the ever-present scrim matches of battle became muted, far off in the distance. In the stillness, their footsteps seemed to resound like stomping elephants, close noises becoming amplified, while the world at large muffled into a strange mysterious "beyond."

Bessy peered between the trees, seeking to view first those she felt sure sought them. Were they being pursued? She felt hunted, as though on borrowed time. Would the soldiers be satisfied that she had fled Boston, or would they take the time to chase her down? When they returned to their home and found them all gone, what had they done? Was she important enough to follow? For sure, they would have caught them by now on horse, compared to their slow pace by foot.

Perhaps her imagination was getting the better of her in weariness. Had her part in Garrett's escape garnered enough attention to warrant an example made for those who would try to do the same for their own captured family members? The tales told by Marie-Kelly, though outlandish, would house a kernel of truth enough to provide word to those wanting to know.

"Oh, God," she whispered, swiping the sticky curls from her forehead, sweat trickling down her spine.

Why hadn't she seen to the safety of her family?

She'd put everyone she held dear in peril.

Her steps faltered, and she tripped.

Malcolm, a pace or two behind, moved quickly to her side, hand at her elbow.

"You okay, Ma?"

Bessy tapped his forearm. "Yes, yes," she replied. "Lost in thought, and I wasn't paying attention."

Standing at a level height with her, his eyes searched her face. She prayed she retained impassive features. He need not be burdened by her fears.

He nodded and allowed her to continue on, leading.

Facing forward, continuing on the track that could have been a food path or a deer trail, she pushed her palm against her abdomen. Had she had any food in her belly, she felt sure she would have had to stop to vomit.

Focusing her attention, she watched for landmarks. They needed to reach a place called Rockland. Garrett especially liked the spot because of the many coastal islands, great for evading or hiding his ship. She suspected he also used one of the islands to off-load supply and cargo.

Just as she managed to quell the anxiety which threatened to paralyze her, the ever-caustic Esther, who had been so compliant and agreeable at the start of their journey, had now taken to a cacophony of grunts and sighs. Whenever they stopped, she complained bitterly of the lack of food, her failing health, sore bones, and how her daughter could have gotten mixed up with such a crowd.

"How do we know our menfolk will even find us at this farm?"

"We don't, Mama," Marie-Kelly responded. "But for sure, we will be safer there than having stayed behind."

The old woman snorted, and Bessy felt the tension rolling off Mackenzie, who had his father's level of patience—close to none—even without looking over her shoulder to his profile. So much like his father, Mack would keep quiet for only so long, and then once the temper was lost, he would give little care to their present situation. Malcolm, on the other hand, more like herself, could be relied upon to hold himself to himself until a measure of safety allowed for a flood of release. When he was younger, this usually resulted in many sleepless nights. Neither outcome was preferable at this moment.

"And what of the bairns having nothing in their bellies? We didn't prepare to be gone so long, floundering in circles." Esther's nasal voice grew higher in pitch. "Perhaps they won't have the strength to carry on."

Bessy turned when she heard the thud of feet. Mackenzie dropped the little girl he was holding to the ground and was in the process of swinging around to face the old woman when a blast blew the top off a tree no more than five feet away.

Maggie screamed and ran to her mother.

Marie-Kelly yelped and grabbed her daughters, holding their heads close to her breast. Malcolm, on her heels, scurried them into the brush and down flat, then turned to his mother, beckoning her forward.

Bessy too grabbed Mack's hand and dropped to the ground. Heart hammering, she listened intently. The crackle of a rifle volley permeated the mist, and bark flew from nearby trees. Surely the scream had given them away. Whoever shared the passage of this stretch of woods would now know they were not alone.

They moved on their hands and knees to the brush, looking behind at Esther.

"By the lord Jesus Christ," came Esther's words in a feral moan.

Malcolm squeezed Bessy's arm, released his hold, then scampered to Esther and dragged her into their huddle.

"Quiet now," he said in a firm voice.

Mack reached into his boot and drew from it a dagger, having had no time to take firearms with them. Bessy did the same, and with a quick glance saw Malcolm draw his own blade.

"'Tis all we have," Mack hissed, round eyes belying his confident tone. "Let's get into the denser bush with the missus and children."

With her heart in her mouth, unable to draw breath, Bessy nodded. Crab fashion, almost like a unit, they moved to surround Marie-Kelly and the girls.

As suddenly as they began, the shots ceased. Cocking her head this way and that, straining as she might, she couldn't detect voices or army order. Surely there would be the noise of many feet. After a few more minutes of trying to determine the more immediate terror—discovering the source of the violence or waiting to be found—action seemed the only course.

With a mouth as dry as dust, she whispered, "We don't know why they are firing, or even if it *is* at us." She swallowed hard. "It could have been a stray bullet from a hunter."

At her older son's expression of incredulity, so much like his father's, she shook her head. "I know. We can either remain as we are or try to move."

Marie-Kelly hadn't taken her arms from around her children. "How could they even know? Surely if they were tracking us, they'd just surround us. There'd be no reason to shoot at children."

"I'll go," Mackenzie declared, making to get to his feet.

Bessy grabbed his arm and shook her head. "No."

She blinked several times. For a moment, she so vividly saw Garrett, she had to remind herself this boy was but sixteen, and bravery and the need to impress flowed through his veins as thick as his own life blood.

"No." She repeated the bare whisper, straining to make her voice heard but not overheard. "No, son. I'll go."

His blue-eyed gaze bore into hers. "You can't—"

"I can and I will," she said and scanned the other faces in their tight circle. Terror wafted off them like a palpable smell. She squeezed Mackenzie's arm. "If they are after me, I need you to see the rest to safety. No one would shoot an unarmed woman. Not even in these times."

She had to stop, her breath fluttering in short spurts. Tears had welled in Malcolm's eye, and she fought back her own response. "If I'm caught, you know where to go. Find your father. He will bargain for my release." Then she forced a smile. "I'll be right back."

"It's the not knowing," Marie-Kelly chimed in.

"But I'm the man," Mackenzie said.

"And," she stressed, taking a moment to pull her children to her. "That's why I need you to ensure everyone makes it to Roger's and then to McCann's farm."

"But—"

"Do as I ask," she said, gaining her feet. "Your father would expect you to do as I say. Look at the watch," she bade him. "Half an hour only. If I'm not back, you carry on. Being a man means accepting this responsibility I lay at your feet. Tell me you are strong enough to see it through."

She wrenched off her wedding ring and handed it to Malcolm. "Hold it for me."

She watched her sons' transition into men before her eyes as their spines straightened and their shoulders squared. They nodded as a unit, and she turned her back on them to face whatever came next.

Chapter Twenty

Bessy scurried to the closest tree and peered around the rough bark. Seeing and hearing nothing, she prayed as she progressed from the shelter of one chestnut tree to another. The foliage had fallen from the boughs, and she relied upon the sheer density to provide cover.

Faintly she picked up sounds of mustering. The area appeared populated with birch, beech, and chestnut, with spruce and juniper peppered in between. She couldn't get close enough to the evergreens for concealment and so stuck to the softwoods. Mist soaked her already damp cloak, and the fog seemed to swirl, ghostly, as she moved ever closer to the noise of stamping feet.

At one point the sounds seemed to surround her like the fog, and she froze, unable to move forward farther. She braced her back against the trunk and forced air in and out of her lungs, and repeated the process until the lightness in her head subsided. In her mind, she recited the Lord's prayer, that the fog would remain to shelter her and her loved ones she'd left hidden. The thought of her family in peril gave her strength.

Her visibility reduced in the thickening fog, she could hardly see the trees she'd just left. Like an insulator, it was, and she lost the compass of her hearing. Where were they? She could no longer detect the clamor of men and feared she imagined sounds. Unbelievable, she chided herself and bit her lip, as she had no plan. She knew only she must protect the children, Marie-Kelly, and the old woman.

So weary was she from her journey that anger Garrett should be here to protect them flared, bringing heat to her chilled skin. A saner side of her being knew her husband wasn't to blame, but in that moment, she could spit flames in her rage against everyone and anyone who stood between her family and safety.

Squatting down, her back firmly against the trunk, she peered around the base of the tree, willing her sight to see through the brush. She felt blind. She glanced behind her, all the while listening, concentrating. How long since she left to skitter through the brush? If she couldn't hear the children and the ancient one's complaints, then the chances were good neither could the soldiers. If that were the case, perhaps she need not concern herself and should return to them.

Her hand patted the deep pocket along her thigh, recalling the gold pocket watch, a family heirloom she'd given to Mackenzie as they set out. They'd left much behind, likely to never see any of it again. She needed to ensure something, however small, carried on.

She closed her eyes and recalled how, with reverence, he'd opened the timepiece, Malcolm watching over his shoulder as he ran a forefinger over the inscribed words:

"If our time together be brief or long, that we mark it as happy." ~Saraid

"My great-grandmother," Bessy said, sad she'd never met the legendary lady.

"Half an hour, only," she had told Mackenzie. Now without any timepiece of her own and time stretching like eons, she had no idea how long she'd been hesitating.

Would it have been better to direct her kin to make for the coast? She hadn't even told them McCann's story and had no way to ensure they would be safe now.

"My God, what have I done—"

She covered her mouth with both hands to fight back a panicked sob.

No, all would be well. She had to believe it to be true and recalled Marie-Kelly's words as she pulled the children closer into the dense brush. "Your da and my Brian know we had to flee. They will come for us. They will find us, no matter what."

A cracking branch close by caused a lurch in her stomach, and she returned to the present, her breath hitched. She visualized men's stealthy movements, picturing the area. She'd been alone so much these last months, constantly on alert, the exercise wasn't a stretch of her imagination.

No longer relying on sight, Bessy squeezed her eyes tightly closed again. There. The insulation of the low-lying cloud had lifted, and the sound of leaves under multiple feet intensified. The rush of the wind through the treetops couldn't disguise the movement of a platoon of bodies traveling beneath their canopy.

Concern over the passage of time fled as she recognized the harsh tones of that black-hearted Lieutenant Samuel Holden—the man who had taken such relish in whipping her Garrett. She wouldn't ever forget the snarl of his face as she pulled Garrett away from his ready whip to flee to the ship, nor the hatred which penetrated the distance.

Not only were they headed in her general direction, but even if they skirted her, they'd find her family in no time at all. Had the boys followed her instructions and left? Surely she'd been gone too long, by this point. All she could do was provide a distraction to allow their escape.

She straightened to standing and no longer needed to strain her hearing. She had imagined they were trying to be stealthy in their approach and realized now that was a result of weather and nothing more. The heavy footfalls were not attempting to conceal their progress. They'd be upon her shortly, and her mind blanked.

"May the saints preserve us," she whispered. Feeling the rough bark along her spine, she pushed her fingers across her stubbled scalp. The memory of how she'd hacked off her locks to find Garrett in the first place gave her courage. Bending, she dug beneath the undergrowth, not knowing what she was digging for until she grasped a rock, which filled her palm.

She had a blade and a rock. She glanced at both and almost laughed at their inadequacy. Never underestimate what you can do with what you have, she reminded herself.

Not taking the time to think it through, she reared up and tossed the stone in the direction opposite to the way she had come, throwing as hard as she could. Hearing it strike bark, the sound seeming to reverberate off every tree in the copse, she smiled.

The steady progression of the militia stalled, and indistinct orders were barked.

She gathered another stone. Smaller than the last, but perhaps she could toss it farther. Arching her arm back as far as the joint would allow, she threw with all her might in a slightly different direction. The distant thwack came as a welcomed report.

Elation at creating a ruse spurred her actions. Encouraged, she bent, straightened, and repeated the motion as she pitched and propelled everything she could bring to hand—until her arm was caught from behind and yanked up the small of her back.

A hand across her mouth prevented her scream. For this she was glad. Banking on her family already on the move, she didn't want the sound of her distress causing the boys and her family to return. They needed to stay together and get to safety. Garrett would come. She knew it to be true. Could feel it in the very marrow of her bones.

Manhandled backward on her feet, wrist held in a vise-like grip by her captor, she declined to struggle. She allowed her limbs to go limp. A woman alone within a circle of men, retaining her wits would be her only weapon. She'd seen soldiers in their many forms during her journey, tending their injuries, seeing the damage of war both physically and mentally, and knew it took little to tip the balance between sanity and insanity in the heat of the moment.

Her head unbound caused one of the men to point and laugh.

"'Tis no lassie," he jeered.

Another peered closer. "No old crone, neither." His leering grin loosened her bowels, and she feared she'd soil herself in her terror. Tobacco-stained teeth stood like sentries amongst the gaps in his mouth when he smiled.

"A gift from the gods, are ye," her captor

whispered in her ear, his sour breath fanning her face. "Something to break the dullness of this never-ceasing march."

Bessy clamped her jaw and steadied her racing heart, as she hung her head, glancing covertly around the assemblage. All the time these men wasted with her meant greater distance for her family. Safety for her sons and the others.

As a matron and healer, she was no fool. She'd tended enough women, seen men in action, listened when Garrett spoke of the discipline to keep his men in line, to know what would befall her if she were not clever. Rethinking her position, she straightened her spine, squared her shoulders, lifted her chin, and speared each man within sight with a direct look.

Snakelike, a hand reached out and grabbed her face, pushing her cheeks hard to pinch against her teeth. "Look at this," he said wobbling her hard. "She's a feisty one, lads. She's got the green-eyed look of a witch. There'll be no tiring her out after once or twice."

A ruckus of agreement made Bessy shift for better footing, bracing her feet shoulder-width apart, readying for impact or potential flight. She might know their intent, but she wouldn't be a willing victim. Garrett had taught her more than a few survival techniques, and she fully intended they'd feel her mark upon them and hoped one or two would walk with a limp before she fell.

"Enough."

The command, though not loud, arrested the men instantly. The leering crowd around her stepped back and gave leave for their superior to enter the circle.

As she feared, Lieutenant Samuel Holden marched

to within an arm's length of her and took his time scrutinizing her from head to toe.

"Mrs. Garrett McGuire, at last," he said, folding his hands behind his back, adopting the relaxed military pose. With his legs spread, his shoulders under his military insignia remained rigid, ready to jump into action. "We've been looking for you."

When she declined to respond, he continued. "You, my dear..." He drew the word out as an endearment, though the steel in his dark eyes allowed for no such illusion. "You denied me your husband's company, and he has something that doesn't belong to him."

The click of several rifle hammers surrounded them in that moment, and the hair on the back of Bessy's neck stood to attention.

"And you," said a voice she knew, yet didn't, as it filled the small clearing, "have something infinitely more valuable of mine."

Chapter Twenty-One

What bizarre twist of fate had led him to pinpoint their location, he refused to question. Like some mystic of old, her need of him drew him to her. She was his compass, and despite the questioning glances from his crew, he followed his gut through the fog and mist. He'd known to the marrow of his bones he would find his family this day. Garrett had off-loaded a few of his men on the island of Monhegan with their windfall, to both lighten the load and protect their future in the event of capture. Careful of the shallows and shoals, he and the remainder of the crew had then maneuvered the great ship past Cape Bessy, which seemed no coincidence, and up the narrow strait until they approached the great cliffs he remembered so well.

With a minimal crew on board to guard the ship, a band of ten set out on foot. If all went as well as his flimsy plan allowed, all would be reunited, in addition to his and Brian's family, by the next morning.

Upon reflection, he discerned the gunfire which elicited the unholy scream and alerted him to Bessy's location also announced the presence of an American platoon. He and his men had flown through the brush as silently as possible, while the low cloud cover and fallen leaves not yet crisp underfoot masked their rush.

As he stood facing the man who'd humiliated him and now held his wife's life in his hands, Garrett hardened his stare, his gaze never wavering from Holden while he prayed the tremble of his stomach didn't reverberate up to his vocal cords. He could almost smell the lust of these soldiers, intent on rape. He clenched his jaw, and the ache of the muscle felt good. The stretch of newly healed welts on his back sharpened his rage with the pain. That the object of their impulse focused on his wife made him almost insane. With tremendous effort he forced the murderous impulse aside.

Garrett chanced a glance at his wife. Even with her clothes stained and hanging from her too-thin frame, face scratched, oozing blood from the jagged brush, and hair shorn, she was beautiful. There was never another like her. She stood so bravely, facing these odds. He quelled the rush of emotion. Her eyes consumed her face, bright at seeing him, and a single tear trickled across the tracks of mud.

The toes on his right foot curled in anticipation of dropping to one knee. He knew, like no other, what the resolute pose of her straight back and clenched fist meant. Her head gave a slight shake, and his bowels went near to watery. He needed to convey that their children were safe—or at least in good hands and on their way to the ship—but had no means. He would have to trust that she would already know.

Quickly, he shifted his disgusted regard back to Holden and raised his eyebrows, expectantly. "Unarmed women now?" Garrett sneered. "Been outmatched too many times to take on real men any longer?"

A quirk lifted the edge of Holden's mouth. "I see you've recovered."

"Sufficiently," Garrett said with a nod, never altering the trim of his gun.

"You'll hang for this, McGuire."

"Unlikely." He prayed his face remained impassive. "You've tried before."

"Your wife—" Holden reached and grasped Bessy by the neck, his fingers easily encircling the slender, pale skin. "For her part, she'll join you, this time."

"You're ill-equipped for threats. You've not the upper hand here." Garrett didn't alter the direction of his stare but prayed too there were no more men waiting in ambush. "You harm her, you all die."

At this, Holden stood so Bessy partly shielded his body. Her petite frame placed her head directly in line with the soldier's heart. "Come now, McGuire. You're supposed to be one of us, after all. A man for all sides, as I understand. The top bidder gets your loyalty for a day or week, or until the money runs low, is it?" He tsked and raised his chin. "Come, now. Give us what you took, and perhaps we can negotiate."

"Any man who would use a woman as a shield is, indeed, no man at all," he snarled, refusing the bait. "I took back what was mine."

Holden laughed, his cheek lifted fractionally, but color stained his ruddy complexion.

"Must I remind you, in case you missed it on our last meeting, The *Isle Sky* is and will remain a free merchant ship. The cargo—whether from that black-hearted Napoleon or from the King himself—belongs to those who commissioned it in the first place."

"There you are mistaken." Holden took a step, seemed to recall Bessy, and reassembled himself. "A British citizen, you responded when your motherland called."

"A free American vessel."

"No more."

"You're Goddamned right no more. My ship's no more British than she is American now, and her cargo and trade belong to neither." Garrett spat the words, incensed every time he considered how both sides pressed free men, whether farmers or tradesmen or those employed on other ships into service, as though prisoners at the whim of this bloody battle. The thought made him ashamed how even he'd been talked into servitude. No more. Not after what he'd seen on sea and land alike, with the Americans being no better than the British they fought for the same reason, as they too used the distraction of political disagreement to invade Canada and try to lay claim to lands not for taking.

"You've struck a deal with the French." Holden's words seemed to gush from his lips unbidden. "Napoleon will not last."

"French, ha." Garrett spat to the side, keeping his eyes level. "Never. We are agreed on that much."

How fate had woven her silvery threads. It seemed so long ago now when he'd chosen a side, which at the time seemed like no side at all, with no choice in the consideration. Neither British nor American. Yet here he stood with a future for himself and his men laid out for them, if they could only make it through this last skirmish.

The shuffle of feet made the discontent of men ready for battle known. Before long, one or the other would take matters into their own hands. They were but heartbeats away from losing the advantage. He'd seen it happen, and then he'd have no guarantee his Bessy would be unscathed.

His voice hardened further. Could he talk Holden around? Was it even worth a try, to ensure her safety? He drew a deep, steadying breath. "I followed orders, nothing more. One side to another—while each lied and cajoled. I've run errands for the Americans because the King said so, I've run for the British for the same reasons, leaving the death of innocents in the wake."

"Well, your country demands you give us what we ask. The guns, the cannon, the bullion." Holden sneered, eyes narrowed, looking triumphant, still gripping Bessy by the neck, shaking her a bit like a rag doll. It was then Garrett noticed the blade in her palm, running up the inside of her arm. "Fair trade, don't you think?"

The gun already cocked, Garrett dropped to one knee and pulled the trigger, his movement fluid. Taking his cue, Bessy too went limp and dropped, while the knife twisted and landed where she hammered it home in the meat of the man's thigh.

The shot took Holden in his left shoulder, and his upper body recoiled to bounce against the tree, while his legs remained where Bessy still held the knife. Her focus turned to her husband and she screamed his name, "Garrett."

Off balance, Holden managed a shot. The bullet strayed off its intended course, striking a sapling on level with Garrett's ear. Then followed a shout, and the air became acrid with the stench of gunpowder and blood, the sounds of direct gunfire deafening.

Through the thickening fog and smoke, Garrett watched Holden scramble for Bessy, who resolutely resisted his tugs to gain her feet. Squinting through diminished visibility, Garrett reloaded shot, took careful aim on the moving target, and fired.

He didn't wait to see if he'd been successful. On hands and knees, he crossed the distance separating him from his wife. Drawing near, his hands squashed in thickened ooze from which the ironized smell announced blood.

"Oh, my love," he breathed, rushing on. Had his worst fears come to fruition? Had a bullet taken her as well? "No. No. No!"

He lurched forward and found her, balled on the ground, hands covering her head. Blood coated her side. "Are you hurt?" He pulled her to him. "Tell me. Speak to me. Bessy? My Bessy!"

A sudden silence seemed to echo louder than the recent gunfire. The skirmish was over. Who won? He didn't care, if he'd lost his beloved. He could face anything but that.

"Garrett," she said, her voice a hoarse whisper.

Then her arms were about his neck, her hands flinging aside his cap as she dug her fingers into his hair. "You found us," she whispered, her lips covering his. "I knew you would."

Her frame, as he pulled her to him, seemed close to skeletal. He swore that in their new home he would take better care of her. Should they survive, he would treasure his greatest prize. "Are you hurt?"

She winced while his hands trailed along her shoulders, down her sides.

"Where, Bessy? Tell me."

"I'm fine, Garrett." She shook her head. "We must get the children. Marie-Kelly and the bairns. They are waiting."

"No, love." His palms cradled her cheeks. "They are fine. Our Mackenzie told me where you'd gone. You foolish, stubborn woman. When will you learn to leave the battles to men?"

Her back straightened, and she pulled back from him, her finger pointed. "When you learn battles are not only fought with guns. The battle of the home front while we wait and wonder—holding on with but a hope and prayer to the Almighty while you traipse off on your adventures—"

Garrett gripped her shoulders, ignored her cry of pain, and kissed her deeply with a pent-up passion he hadn't realized needed release.

Releasing her, gratified of her breathless silence, he pulled her to him again. "The children are fine. On their way to the ship."

He stood, drawing her up with him.

Her arms encircled his waist as she buried her face in his coat. "Oh, Garrett!" Her words were muffled by the fabric. "I was so scared. I had nothing. Could think of nothing but to distract them from our family."

"And fearful I am sure you will remain, until we are out of these treacherous waters. We are amongst foes on all sides, and you need tending, my darling."

"Captain, Sir." A tap on his shoulder made him look around, finally taking a moment to survey the carnage. Two of his men limped, supported by others, while all around lay strewn the soldiers.

Bessy pulled away. "They need tending."

"We need to go," the young seamen said. "None of our men sustained grievous injury."

"How many dead?" he asked.

"Only Holden and another. What shall we do with

the wounded?"

"Disarm and leave them. They'll be found soon enough. We must make haste."

"After I see to their wounds," Bessy declared, moving around the circle.

"No—"

"Yes," she said with the tone of iron, and he knew she wouldn't be dissuaded. "We are not barbarous. They will be set to rights, and then we can leave. There's no telling how long they will have to wait until someone stumbles across them, in this weather."

Chapter Twenty-Two

Not until she began tending the wounded did she realize the blood coating her clothing was not just Holden's. Bessy hadn't moved fast enough. The first bullet that struck Holden in the shoulder had first passed through her bicep. No bone breakage, that she could tell. That she knew Holden to be shot also confirmed no spent cartridge to dislodge.

The blood seeped down her arm, but she worked quickly tending the others so her party could be off. Ripping a section of cloth from her cloak, she made a makeshift bandage. Little injury had been sustained by Garrett's few men.

As much as she tried to brazen out against the searing pain, the wound burned as though a hot poker, direct from the coals, had been implanted into her arm. She'd treated plenty of gun wounds over the years, but this was the first she had met for herself the actual numbing agony. Each step through the thick bush jarred and sent lightning-like aches along every nerve ending. Her jaw clenched as she fought to keep pace, eager to be reunited with her family.

Despite the applied pressure, she could feel the blood spurt and be caught but not held by the saturated rags tied to her upper arm under her cloak. She had managed to conceal the bandage from Garrett while he attended his men and planned their next moves. But if this bleeding continued, he was sure to notice, and that would only serve to slow them down, to perhaps be trapped by another ambush, for she doubted Holden had operated with only such a small party of men. They were running against the clock again.

The thick, musk-smelling fluid now coursed down her arm to pool at the elbow she cradled close to her chest, where it soaked through the thick cloth of her cloak into the palm of her hand. She felt lightheaded and woozy, pacing each stride as though intoxicated. She muttered an oath and shook her head to clear the static of drowsiness that threatened to consume her. If only they could lessen the pace, or stop for water, but no time could be wasted. She needed to be reunited with her family, and they needed to get safely to the ship and be on their way. Where there was one militia group, there would be another. As Garrett said, they were surrounded by enemies, for no one considered "their" side—the Canadian side—friend.

Fledgling, like a newly born colt, Canada was finding its own independence from Britain. Too new a country to be taken seriously, the Americans seemed to consider those of the north a mere branch of their own history, with territory to be taken while England occupied themselves with Napoleon.

Garrett's dual occupation as emissary between British and American traders gave him a bird's-eye view of the goings-on. And so they had chosen—not to choose one or the other, but an alternative. For the McGuires, the MacLeods, and those who would follow them, Canada would be their home by choice, and they would defend that choice with their very lives, if need be. She would see her children raised free of this constant conflict.

If they could find their way. This last leg of the journey. To be so close... Yet weeks of exhaustion were catching up with her, and she stumbled over her own feet, catching her balance and marching on.

The thoughts of freedom and a fresh start gave her strength. She positioned herself to walk where her injured arm faced away from Garrett's view. She hugged the limb closer, bit her lip to mask the grimace, and strode on.

Garrett glanced back at her over his shoulder while he marched next to her brother in tight conversation. His face was stern, set, focused. His hand reached out to touch her, but she was just out of his grasp. "You're as white as a sheet. Allow me to carry you."

She glared at him. "And slow us down further?" The words crunched out between tight lips much harsher than she would have liked. Summoning a rage in place of the fear she experienced was the only thing keeping the pain and bleary vision at bay. She couldn't—no, she wouldn't let them down.

They'd been each other's companion for too many years for him not to recognize when to shelve his own opinions. He nodded, but she watched the muscle of his jaw tighten and flex as he turned his face away to resume his discussion with Brian.

The flavor of salt in the air dewed on her tongue, and all at once the ocean seemed to open before them. The cover of trees came to an end, and their band stood as one on the cliff overlooking a rocky beach below. Shrouded in an apron of mist, the *Isle Sky* seemed to float above the steel gray water where constant white-capped waves moved against it, yet held it in place. The brown hue of the hull stood as the only solid in an equally dreary sky void of the sun's penetration. The line between sky and ocean blurred.

"At last," she muttered, catching her breath which wheezed in and out, searing her lungs.

Bending slightly at the waist, she scanned first one way, then the other. She couldn't spot even a deer trail leading down through the thick fog.

Cannon fire penetrated the air, and she started. "The children, Garrett. Where are the children?"

The men had their arms at the ready, and Garrett drew her closer to his side. "Be still," he commanded. "They should already be on board." He bent to one knee and peered to the vessel. "Yes, there. See? The signal."

She had no idea what he referenced but could only shake her head, trusting him to know.

"Where's the cannon fire coming from? I cannot see another ship, Garrett." She turned to watch his face, set like a hawk's, scanning the horizon. "Are they firing on the *Isle Sky*?"

He shook his head, though he didn't turn from his searching of the skyline. "I think not. Sounds farther out. Brian? What say you?"

Brian had stepped up to Bessy's other side. "Aye," he replied, while he too searched for the source of the weaponry. "We'd better make haste and be aboard while there's still cover."

Men used to unsteady decks and slippery surfaces, they descended the steep incline as a goat would a rocky pasture. Bessy, by contrast, slipped and slid with each attempt.

Another volley of gunfire sounded, closer still, and

Garrett cursed. He picked her up bodily and flung her over his shoulder as though she were a sack of flour. Unexpectedly, the sudden shock on her injured arm caused her to both scream and flail to protect the injury from further assault.

He paid no attention. In actuality, he seemed to take this as protest to being carried rather than an exclamation from pain.

"For the love of Christ, woman," he yelled. "Don't be so stubborn."

She ached to find the words to rebuke him for his blasphemy, but as she'd done little better these last days and the pain had stolen her ability to either breath or talk, she bit the inside of her cheek to prevent further exclamations.

When he set her down upon the rocks, her vision had narrowed to a single point of light, and she swayed. The muscles of her legs refused to obey, and she felt herself going down as her legs buckled under her.

"Bessy, love!" Garrett grabbed her shoulders and drew his hand away quickly to see the thick smear of her blood that now coated his palm. "Bessy, no!"

Chapter Twenty-Three

Bessy woke heaving. Searing pain scorched her brain. White hot knives of torture flowed along her limbs. Nausea overwhelmed her. Saliva filled her mouth, and her stomach pushed bile while she gasped for breath, nose clogged.

Hands held her, soothing. A wet cloth bathed her face. As soon as she could draw stale air, the acrid smell of gunpowder choked her again and combined with the rocking of the ship to have her stomach heaving again. She curled her body into a tight ball and gagged into the basin at her cheek. She couldn't take the constant motion. She must be still. Her brain swam, and she couldn't get steady. Sudden lurches tossed her back and forth, bumping her from one surface to another.

"Try a little water."

It was Marie-Kelly's sweet voice.

Bessy tried to open her eyes, but the room swirled, causing her to retch again. The room inverted, and bright lights flashed at the edge of her vision. She squeezed them tight, until her muscles ached, and she tried to concentrate on Marie-Kelly's presence. What torturous hell had they fallen into?

"The children?" She managed to form the words over the swelling dryness of her tongue. Try as she might, she couldn't concentrate enough to take an internal assessment of her health.

"Here," her friend confirmed. "With us. All safe."

Bessy felt a loosening of the band of anxiety that gripped her heart. But her stomach heaved and bobbed like a stray cork on tossing waves. "For the love of all that is holy," she whispered.

"What, my dearest?" Marie-Kelly asked. "I cannot make out yer words." She continued, "Yes, they are safe. Can you hear me?"

Bessy inched her fingers across the blanket to reached for Marie-Kelly's hand. Finding the cool fingertips, she squeezed.

"Though where 'here' is, I could hardly know," Marie-Kelly's voice continued, close to her ear. "But the men will see us safe. Of that I am sure. You need not worry. Just be well, dearest."

Bessy could only nod, then heaved again. There was nothing to come up. The dryness made her gag until her face felt like it would explode with the pressure. The pitching of the ship and the violent slap of the waves against the hull left her little room but to concentrate on the ceaseless lurch of her stomach.

Awakening to her surroundings, and with her eyes shut against the dizziness, her hearing became acute. The stamping of many boots overhead, the shouting of orders, the creaking of the oak as the ship was made to heel. Then the door burst open, and with it came fresh air. She jumped at the intrusion but wasn't able to move. The salty dew seemed to clear the stench of her sickness in an instant, bringing a welcomed relief.

"I have but a moment," Garrett's voice boomed in the small cabin. "How is my wife?"

He was beside her and took her in his arms. She

felt the cradle of his embrace and his lips upon her hair.

"The wound has been cleaned and the flow of blood stanched. She vomits with the toss of the ship, but that cannot be helped." Marie-Kelly could be heard from a slight distance. "Our Bessy is conscious now, and I feel she will strengthen to rights as she always does."

A small pause and Bessy tried to open her eyes. Unable to accomplish even this small feat without succumbing to the retching, she instead felt for his hands on her and squeezed them with the little strength she could muster.

"That's it, my love. That's it. God willing, as you always do." His voice came hoarse.

Before she could manage the herculean task of sight, his arms had left her, stomping on floorboards resounded, and the door banged shut, leaving the air stifled again. Exhaustion overcame her, and she allowed the blackness to sway her into its midst.

Unsure of the passage of time, Bessy became aware of her surroundings again and arched her head to hear. She needed to focus. With all her concentration, she turned her head and opened her eyes. Sighting her friend, she rallied her voice. "Tell me, Marie-Kelly. Tell me what has happened. Are we in battle?"

"No, praise God, we are not."

"The smell?"

"My dearest friend, it is but a miracle granted by the shroud of the weather. We pass close by but have as yet to be recognized as we make our way through the many channels and out to the open sea."

Bessy tossed her gaze this way and that, not comprehending, wanting to gain her own feet beneath her and ascertain the situation for herself, immediately. Reliance on vague information became frustrating so quickly.

"Shush, my dear," Marie-Kelly said, placing gentle hands against her chest to push her back into the cushions. "I will tell you."

"Then quickly, for I have little patience and must know."

"My Brian related the names of the ships as they spotted them as soon as we came to the beach, for these two enemies made no effort to conceal their intent to one another. The captain instructed a wide berth to steer clear of their target, but we were deep into the many forks of land and needed to gain open sea to be fully free."

"How?"

"Shush now, and I will tell all I know."

With great effort, Bessy swallowed back the resurgence of bile and buried her impatience.

"They found us at Pemaquid Point."

"Yes, yes," Bessy muttered. "So we were not far from McCann's farm. We had made it."

"That we did, my dearest. You saw us straight, indeed," agreed Marie-Kelly. "But the *USS Enterprise* was close at hand there, as well. Brian thinks it is quite the miracle the *Isle Sky* was not spotted by them, as he is sure Holden and his crew were transported there by the very same."

Bessy gasped and lifted her heavy hand to her face. "Indeed."

Bessy could imagine, rather than see, the confirmation of Marie-Kelly's facial features.

"But the *Enterprise* must have been pursued by the

British brig *HMS Boxer*, who didn't hesitate to engage," Marie-Kelly continued.

"No," Bessy gasped. Her hands had dropped to grip her midsection, muscles clenched. A distant boom alerted her that they were not out of danger yet. At any moment their luck could change and they would be spotted and—no, she couldn't think of it.

"That's none so close as it was," Marie-Kelly soothed, brushing the cloth across Bessy's forehead. "When the fog swirled and the rain started in earnest, I could even see them from the porthole. Blessed be all that is holy, I near fainted from the fear."

Bessy found the strength to focus her blurry sight on her friend.

"Yes." Marie-Kelly nodded her head vigorously, cupping Bessy's cheeks. "There you are now. I knew such a wound would not hold you down for long."

"Tell me," Bessy said. "I cannot bear the suspense. Why do I still hear the guns?"

"We are slow to maneuver at only half mast, keeping close to the shore while we tack into the foggy mist rather than through it. We need to retain the cover, you see. My Brian said if we are quiet and let the current take us, we will be clear without notice."

Bessy could only nod. Could such a maneuver really work? She prayed that these men knew their trade, and that their tactics would do as they expected.

"Brian says the two men-of-war are well matched and circling decisively, each firing intentionally. They have each other to focus upon. Each have eighteen-pound carronades. The *Enterprise* is well equipped with two nine-pound long guns, and at least a hundred and two men, while the *Boxer* has two six-pounders." She paused to wipe her own face.

"I had no idea you knew so much about these things, my dear old friend."

Marie-Kelly caught the jest and smiled. "I am good. Do you not think of retaining what's important to survival at the time? That I could but forget what I was told of those blasted guns, but I fear it is seared into my mind now, and though I know little of what they mean, I am assuming it is no good news unless we escape."

"On that I can agree."

"All those men. To be so close to land. It is terrible, my Bessy. I could but watch a moment, though it seems like the battle has raged for hours. I feel I shall never see anything else in my memory again."

Bessy patted her friend's hand, her strength returning quickly as she recalled the many deaths she'd witnessed on the battlefield, the many severe wounds she had tended on her journey to Garrett.

"Through the mist, I could see men from either ship swimming for the shore," Marie-Kelly continued. "I swear the ships were but a pistol's distance from one another. Brian says they would spare no notice for any other."

"Would they engage on land, do you think?"

"I could not imagine they would be in any fit form." Marie-Kelly shook her head. "We need only to make open water."

At that moment, the creak of the vessel, the slap of the masts, seemed to halt the ship in mid-motion. Then the ship heaved forward and broke through the waves as they gained speed.

Marie-Kelly jumped to the porthole and threw it open. Fresh air billowed in with the spray off the bow.

"We are away," she declared. "We're free, at last."

They smiled at one another.

"At last."

Epilogue

It is said that the War of 1812 was a defining one for the country which became Canada. Had the British not assumed allegiance and taken loyalty for granted without abiding by their promises, had the French not managed to hold to their territory, thereby creating a bridge of the Napoleonic war across the ocean, and had the Americans not used the distraction as an opportunity to invade, pillage, and burn the new capital, all might have been different.

Like all wars, this one began years before 1812, with the build-up of tensions, and carried on much longer than anticipated. During this time, the fledgling country of Canada became populated, at first by explorers, adventurers, runaways, and then sailors avoiding conscription, all those and more seeking a free port and more importantly freedom of opportunity, like our heroes—a new home—a new start.

Within a day, the *Isle Sky* rounded the coast of Nova Scotia, seeing Yarmouth off the port bow. Bessy managed to come on deck, gaining strength through the knowledge her family was safe at last. Assuming her position at the helm, next to her beloved, Bessy could imagine their new home, the settlement they would help forge together.

Garrett reached round to pull her close. "Soon, my love," he whispered. "We will be home soon."

And they were, settling in an area they came to call Steep Creek for the high rocky cliffs which gave way to a protected harbor, previously known as Pirate Harbor, to anchor their ship. Very soon they united with the families of crew which had come ahead and populated the area, making ready.

Next from Lori Power...

Chapter One

1690, Pirate Harbor, Nova Scotia

Fabian Power brushed the moisture from his eyes and scanned the horizon, at times wondering if he'd navigated to the edge of the world. Had he not a lifetime of experience sailing his three-masted *Marie* from England to the Caribbean and north, to these same Godforsaken shores, he might just think so. Yet he knew better. Trusted navigation charts had steered them correctly many times over.

Still, the fog lay so thick, the threat of ambush could be around any of these craggy, rocky turns. Like a thick soup disguising a fish bone, one of the crown's vessels could lie in wait, ready to take him in for the hanging he so rightfully deserved.

A rueful smile lifted his cheeks. Let them try as they had so many times before. He ran light fingers along the sturdy oak rail. His *Marie* was as swift, fast, and loose as the lady she was named for, a long ago love of his youth who'd taught him so much. Who then came to be his wife.

He shook his head to clear the memory. He'd see her again soon. Now was not the time to alter his wits with a longing he couldn't satisfy.

He stood at the helm, listening to the silence on board. The insulated kind of muffled activity that only came with thick cloud cover. A calm that was broken only by the barking seals on a beach he couldn't see. Their sudden noise alerted him to the shore outside his line of sight. There'd be treacherous rocks along the coastline. Running aground here wouldn't be as forgiving as on the sandy Caribbean shores. Here the shale would rip the hull to shreds. The last thing he needed with this cargo would be to run aground.

"Make lively, Matty-boy," he said to his first mate.

In another lifetime, he and Matthew Welsh were fishermen. They grew up as sons of fishermen. Generations of them. The ocean ran deep in their veins. They understood the old ways. When they were of age, they followed their sires, navigating their time between Ireland and the great rock known as Newfoundland. There, they chased a more edible loot—the cod stock.

Until the English interfered by pressing fishermen into soldiers' service.

Fabian's hands fisted with rage at how the Crown had seen the end of that simple way of life and their ability to feed their families. By the sea, of the sea, had been the ways of his family. Given the choice, he wouldn't see his men or their families starve. Instead of fishing, he and Matty took their boats, their knowledge of the currents, tides, and winds, and became men for hire. Now the English saw them as significant adversaries. And well they should.

Another life.

A seabird screeched and dove. The sound of the drop into the water resonating like a boulder in the thick cloud. Fabian pushed the clasp of the compass. A gift from his beloved wife, Marie. The needle swung back and forth like a pendulum until settling as he steadied his hand. He snapped the case closed and marched back to the charts. He discarded his original papers in favor of the latest stolen from a French frigate on route for Louisburg. Finger poised over their last known location, running along the log-line, he drew a straight line, reopened the compass, double-checked the direction, and made a note. They were close. Had to be.

"Drop the lead and line," he yelled.

"Aye, Capt'in."

With a satisfied "plop" the lead dropped into the ocean. Fabian licked his lips. The salt thick, the air briny, served only to make him thirsty. It shouldn't take long for the weight to sink. With the evenly spaced knots, he'd know in a moment how deep they were and by consequence how close to the rugged shoreline.

With a full hold of loot and plunder, their next occupation would be to find a hiding spot—the right spot—to unload, and make ready to sail again. Soon they'd bring their families here to settle where they could own their own land, harvest their own crops. Become fishermen again.

Patience.

The sale of the bounty would come later. The crew were anxious. Too many near misses lately. Fishermen at heart, they lacked the staying power of a life on the run. Yet the French were building a fortress on the island and Fabian's hands itched with the bounty of the imperial wealth enroute. He needed to unload the present cargo to make ready to plunder. One more good haul and they could cast off their black flag and have enough to take care of their families for the rest of their days. Maybe for generations to come.

Wouldn't that be something. A legacy. Wouldn't his ol' da, dead these many years, be shaking his ghostly, near-bald head and smiling.

Just one more.

"Weigh anchor," the boatswain yelled through the mist.

"At last," Fabian whispered and walked to where his old mate stood at the wheel. Then, giving in to his relief, pounded Matt on the back and said louder, "At last."

Just then the fog lifted. Reluctant rays of sunshine splintered through as though coming in haloed rays from heaven. Enough to see the shores. They had tacked significantly closer than he had reckoned. Less than a boat's length away from the nearest visible rock. Jagged shale boulders sat at a depth not far from the waterline. Where the fog cleared, he could see the points breaking the water. What he couldn't see was what creased his brow. They must have released the lead in a drop-off. Any closer than they were and they'd damage the ship.

Though his collar was pulled tight against the chill, the wind stole his breath as he exhaled. Despite the close call, the toothed coastline offered perfect protection, unlike any other they'd encountered before. So many coves for cover. While perfect for an ambush, he felt certain, this offered better protection from detection. Beaches of sand and rock, bordered by enormous boulders from the days of Job provided much needed seclusion.

Fabian turned to Matty. "Find a way ashore." He crossed to the lee side of the ship. "Land ho, you bunch of scallywags."

Matty nodded and lifted the spyglass. "I can see nay but the plume of breaking waves against the thick fog to the north," he said. "Any farther and we run the risk of running aground without clear visibility."

"We see well enough right here," Fabian said and pointed. "Clear sightlines may surely give us away to the devil English, patrolling, yet protect us from them seeing us."

In a collective pause before activity, the crew listened intently for sounds from the land. A village, sea creatures, the breaking waves, all markers for home or hostility. Depending on the shift of the wind, the thickness of the fog would determine their safety. Minutes passed and nothing presented itself. As if on a collective release of pent-up breath, the crew jumped to their assigned tasks.

This wasn't the first time they had hauled loot unseen, but Fabian hoped it would be close to the last.

While the company completed their duties, he retired to his cabin to retrieve a map from the bottom of the pile in a locked drawer. Closing his eyes, then opening them again, he roughed out in detail what he saw of the coast, adding to his ever more detailed map. Then, on a separate sheet in a different drawer, he plotted his location. He stood to peer out the port hole. Yes. A narrow peninsula separated the ocean from a small pond and the land beyond. Perfect. A steep hill overgrown by trees. To the right, cliffs of rock, inlaid with sea caves.

Fabian nodded to himself. "By the holy father, you've seen me come home."

A word about the author…

There's always a story, Lori Power says, and she insists conversation is key. Listening to understand, exploring the concepts, and opening to the adventure is what puts light in the darkness. In fact, there's nothing like a great gab to lead to an idea for the next novel.

Lori's first novel, *Storms of Passion*, was published by The Wild Rose Press under their Champagne line in 2014. Her second novel, *Hit 'n Run*, Book 1 in the "Under Suspicion" series, was published by Limitless Press in 2015 and includes the sequel *The Tables Have Turned*. Then came the "Gentle Surf" series, and now we're pleased to introduce readers to the "McGuire" series, of which this is the third book.

Collaboration is important to improving one's craft, and as such, Lori is an active member of the Romance Writers of America and of the Alberta Romance Writers Association, as well as belonging to both a critiquing group and a beta reading weekly group.

Lori looks forward to continuing to find the good story; hashing out a scene, having fun with a character, and always falling in love with each.

Visit her at:

www.loripowerwriter.com

Thank you for purchasing
this publication of The Wild Rose Press, Inc.

For questions or more information
contact us at
info@thewildrosepress.com.

The Wild Rose Press, Inc.
www.thewildrosepress.com